BEYOND THE STARS

BEYOND THE STARS

Barbara Cartland

Chivers Press • G.K. Hall & Co.
Bath, England   Thorndike, Maine USA

CAR
LARGE
PRINT

This Large Print edition is published by Chivers Press, England and by G.K. Hall & Co., USA.

Published in 1997 in the U.K. by arrangement with Reed Consumer Books.

Published in 1997 in the U.S. by arrangement with The Berkley Publishing Group.

U.K. Hardcover ISBN 0–7451–6956–2 (Chivers Large Print)
U.S. Softcover   ISBN 0–7838–1894–7 (Nightingale Collection Edition)

The text of this Large Print edition is unabridged.
Other aspects of the book may vary from the original edition.

Set in 16 pt. New Times Roman.

Printed in Great Britain on acid-free paper.

British Library Cataloguing in Publication Data available

Library of Congress Cataloging-in-Publication Data

Cartland, Barbara, 1902–
      Beyond the stars / Barbara Cartland.
          p.   cm.
      ISBN 0–7838–1894–7 (lg. print : sc)
      1. Large type books.   I. Title.
[PR6005.A765B4   1997]
823'.912—dc20   96–30936

Author's Note

The most spectacular highlight of the glittering and luxurious celebrations to mark the Diamond Jubilee of Queen Victoria in 1897 was the Devonshire House Fancy-Dress Ball.

On the 2nd July the 8th Duke of Devonshire and his Duchess celebrated the Jubilee in their magnificent house in Piccadilly.

Duchess Louise had, when she first came to England, been an entrancing beauty. She became first the Duchess of Manchester and then later married the Duke of Devonshire.

At her Ball she represented Zenobia, Queen of Palmyra, and was carried into the Ball-Room on a palanquin by a number of bearers.

The Duke was dressed as the Emperor Charles V. He was known to be shy and retiring by nature, but he managed to stay awake during the Ball and did not fall asleep, which was something he frequently did in the House of Lords.

The guests at the Ball represented all the most attractive and exciting Society of the day.

Unfortunately Queen Victoria was too old and infirm to attend after all her many other public appearances during the Jubilee.

Her son, the Prince of Wales, however, was extremely impressive as the Grand Prior of the Order of St John of Jerusalem.

The Duke of Marlborough was magnificent as the French Ambassador to the Court of Catherine of Russia.

The Hon. Mrs George Keppel the acknowledged mistress of the Prince of Wales, was Madame de Polignac. She had taken great care to ensure that every detail of her costume was correct, and she even discovered material that had been made in the eighteenth century.

Some of the costumes were to prove not only uncomfortable, but laughable. The Countess of Westmorland as Hebe wore a huge stuffed eagle on her shoulder which made it extremely difficult to dance.

An American hostess, Mrs Ronalds, representing Euterpe, the Muse of Music, had electric lights arranged in her hair so that they could light up a lyre.

William Cavendish was created Duke of Devonshire in 1694 as a result of his support for William III, and when Berkeley House came up for sale in 1696, it was acquired for the Duke. It became known as Devonshire House until, in 1733, it was destroyed by a disastrous fire. After the fire the Duke lost no time in planning a new residence and William Kent was chosen as the designer.

It was sold by the 9th Duke in 1919, and in 1924 its new owners pulled it down. I remember being entranced by the curving marble staircase with its crystal hand-rail and the garden, which stretched right down to

Berkeley Square.

It was one of the sights of London and it never occurred to anyone then that these beautiful and historic houses should be preserved.

CHAPTER ONE

1897

The Earl of Ardwick stared in astonishment at the very beautiful young woman standing opposite him.

'What do you mean—you are not coming to the Ball?' he asked.

'What I said, Ingram,' she replied, 'is that I am not coming with you.'

'Not coming with me?' the Earl repeated incredulously. 'I do not know what you are talking about.'

Heloise Brook moved slowly towards the window.

She walked with a grace that had been acclaimed by practically every member of the Club in St James's Street.

Even His Royal Highness the Prince of Wales had commented on it.

She was well aware that with her red hair shining in the sun coming through the window, and wearing her emerald green gown, she looked like a goddess.

There was something Eastern and magical about her that aroused a man's passions.

She had heard this said often enough when she wore green.

She had therefore deliberately put on a green

1

gown that accentuated her figure before the Earl arrived.

He waited until she had reached the window before he asked sharply;

'What is this all about? What have I done to upset you?'

'It is not that *I* am upset,' Heloise said in a soft voice, 'it is you, dear Ingram.'

'Of course I am upset when you say you are not coming to the Ball with me, when you made all that palaver about having a very special gown! God knows, it cost enough money!'

'You surely did not begrudge it to me?' Heloise asked.

'I did not begrudge it,' the Earl replied, 'but I thought it a somewhat large expenditure for something you will wear only once.'

Heloise did not answer, and after a moment he went on:

'Anyway, I bought the gown, so what are you complaining about?'

'I am simply trying to tell you, Ingram, that I am not coming to the Ball with you. I have chosen another partner both for the Ball and—for—life!'

The last words came very slowly.

The Earl felt he could not have heard aright.

'For life!' he exclaimed. 'What do you mean by that?'

'I am afraid you will be upset,' Heloise said, 'but I have decided to marry Ian Dunbridge.'

The Earl, who was walking towards her, stopped dead in sheer astonishment.

'Marry Dunbridge?' he questioned. 'I do not believe it!'

Heloise did not speak.

'But—you are engaged to me!' the Earl exclaimed.

'Only secretly, and you agreed that we should think it over before we made it public.'

The Earl seemed for a moment to be lost for words.

Then he said furiously:

'You are marrying Dunbridge because he is a Duke, not because you love him.'

'That is my business,' Heloise answered.

The Earl's voice was sharp as a whiplash as he said slowly:

'You have kept me dangling on the hook because you thought Dunbridge would not "come up to scratch." Now that he has, you are chucking me over, just because you want a superior title!'

Heloise gave a little sigh.

'A Duke is always—a Duke,' she murmured.

'Curse you!' the Earl exclaimed. 'You have made a complete fool of me. All I can say is that I think you have behaved disgracefully and with a complete lack of principle!'

He walked towards the door.

'Goodbye, Heloise,' he said, 'and I hope I never see you again!'

He walked out before she could answer.

With a great effort he managed to close the door quietly, when he wanted to slam it.

As he crossed the hall he could hardly believe that what he had heard was true.

Heloise Brook, whom he had been courting for nearly two months, had turned him down at the last minute.

And all because the Duke of Dunbridge had finally 'taken the plunge.'

'Damn him, and damn all women!' he cursed.

His carriage was waiting outside.

He had brought it with him rather than a vehicle he could drive himself.

He had hoped to bring Heloise back to central London with him.

Her father, Lord Penbrook, had a house at Ranelagh.

Although it might be considered indiscreet, Heloise had on several occasions allowed the Earl to convey her to London, the excuse being a Ball or a dinner to which they had both been invited.

The Earl threw himself onto the back seat.

As he did so, he was aware that a large gown-box had been placed on the seat opposite.

'What is that?' he enquired of the footman.

'Oi were told t'put it in th' carriage with Yer Lordship,' the footman replied.

The Earl's lips tightened. He knew it was the costume that Heloise had intended to wear that

4

night.

They had been going to a Fancy-Dress Ball that the Duchess of Devonshire was giving at Devonshire House.

It was part of the celebrations that were taking place to mark Queen Victoria's Diamond Jubilee.

For months the whole of Society had been preparing for it.

The Duchess had asked everybody to come in Fancy-Dress.

There had been much speculation, arguments, and some disagreeableness about who was to appear as what.

Lady Warburton had made sure before anyone could stop her that she would come as Britannia.

Lady Gerard had chosen Astarte, Goddess of the Moon.

These two had forestalled and disappointed a great number of other aspirants.

Heloise had laid claim that she should be Cleopatra.

Her rivals had reluctantly acceded to her insistence.

It was left to the Earl, therefore, to make himself into a suitable Mark Antony.

Fortunately the costume of a Roman General was distinguished-looking and not too fanciful.

It annoyed him now to think that in her desire to go as Cleopatra, Heloise had been extremely extravagant.

'She was Queen of Egypt,' she had insisted, 'and had the most fantastic jewellery. Think of the fuss that has since been made about the one pearl earring she dissolved in wine to give to Mark Antony!'

'Pearls were the most expensive of jewels in those days,' the Earl replied, 'and as a whole campaign could be fought on the proceeds from one earring, I consider it an unnecessary extravagance.'

'I am sure, dearest Ingram, you will not deny me a pair of pearl earrings,' Heloise said, 'and, of course, we must say we are as we were before I gave you one to drink!'

The Earl had conceded that he should provide pearl earrings.

Of course they were the largest and most expensive obtainable in Bond Street.

He found the gown itself, what there was of it, was on Heloise's instructions also festooned with jewels.

'After all, you can wear it for only one evening,' he said, 'and semi-precious jewels are something you will never wear again.'

'I want to look entirely authentic,' Heloise replied.

The Earl had paid up simply because Heloise was undoubtedly the most beautiful girl he had ever seen.

If he had to marry someone, he was determined that she should be unarguably

6

outstanding.

Heloise, with her red hair, green eyes, and translucent skin, was the most beautiful young woman in the whole of Mayfair.

She had rivals who thought they eclipsed her.

But they were among the married women who were admired by the Prince of Wales and his contemporaries.

It was the Prince who had made it possible for the first time for a Gentleman to have an affair with a woman of his own class without her being ostracised by the rest of the Social World.

Lillie Langtry had been fêted and acclaimed by nearly every important hostess in London.

The Prince then added to the list the Countess of Warwick, with whom he was really in love, the Princess de Sagan, and a number of other Beauties.

Then he was completely and absolutely satisfied with the charm of Mrs Keppel.

The Earl had enjoyed a few fiery *affaires-de-coeur* with exquisitely beautiful married women.

It was only when he saw Heloise Brook that he thought the Ardwick diamonds would look sensational on her red hair.

From that moment he decided it was time, at nearly twenty-eight, that he should settle down.

He would produce an heir, or, rather, several

7

sons to inherit his vast estates.

Extremely rich, the Ardwicks had added to their property generation by generation.

As the 10th Earl, he was one of the greatest Landowners in England.

He found it almost impossible to believe, considering his importance, that the girl he had chosen to be his wife should prefer a Duke.

Now that the Earl thought about it, he remembered Heloise had been slightly piqued when one of her friends had married a Marquess.

It was not, he had thought, an enviable position to be the wife of a man who was twenty years her senior.

At the same time, it was an attractive title.

He guessed how much Heloise disliked the fact that her friend would walk into dinner in front of her.

For Heloise to become a Duchess was certainly 'one in the eye' for every ambitious Mama and eager *débutante*.

They had run after Dunbridge ever since he had left Eton.

It had never occurred to the Earl that the woman he had asked to be his wife would prefer another man simply because of his title.

He would have been very stupid, which he was not, if he had not been aware that he was extremely handsome.

He was also an outstanding sportsman and had been described as the most intelligent of all

8

the younger men at Court.

He ran the estates himself with a brilliance of organisation which was the envy of every other Landowner in the County.

His horses, which again he chose himself, invariably won all the Classic Races.

He was expert at Polo, outstanding in the Hunting Field.

He had won so many Point-to-Points and Steeple-Chases that some men refused to compete with him.

'I am fed up with you romping home ahead of me,' one of them had said to him the previous week. 'It would be so much easier just to give you the Challenge Cup before we start than to exhaust ourselves galloping across country to watch you come in first at the winning-post!'

It was a protest half humourous and half serious.

It made the Earl feel uncomfortable.

He knew, however, that his success was not only due to his riding.

He chose his horses with great care and trained them himself.

His house, Ardwick Park, which had been in his family for generations, was as near perfection as it was possible for him to make it.

After his father's death he had redecorated it, but, to everyone's astonishment, not in the Late Victorian style that was now the vogue.

Instead, he had restored it to how it had

9

looked at the beginning of the century.

Although the Georgian style was out of fashion, the Earl had swept everything away that the Victorians had found so attractive.

Now it looked as it had when the Adam Brothers had finished with it.

Because it was so unusual to do such a thing, people flocked to Ardwick Park to see the alterations its owner had made.

Strangely enough, it was the Prince of Wales who swept away any criticisms by saying:

'You have created for yourself a magnificent background which, I must say, Ardwick, is worthy of you.'

After that, everybody acclaimed Ardwick Park.

They themselves, however, continued with their aspidistras, their antimacassars, and their over-decorated, over-tasselled Reception Rooms.

The Earl had recently been thinking about the changes he would make to the beautiful bedroom that would be Heloise's after their marriage.

He was aware there was too much pink in the carpets and curtains for a woman with her fiery red hair.

He had already planned very carefully the adjustments he intended to make.

He wanted it to be a pleasant surprise for her when she came to Ardwick Park as its Chatelaine.

There were so many things he wanted to give her which he believed would make her even more beautiful than she was already.

It was because he had such generous plans in his mind that he resented her extravagance.

It was for a lot of gaudy nonsense which would never be used again after the Devonshire House Ball was over.

He told himself that there was now no point in his going to the Ball.

Here he was, cluttered with the gown which Heloise had been going to wear.

His own costume was waiting for him at his house in Grosvenor Square.

Like most men, he disliked Fancy-Dress parties.

He knew, however, it always amused women to dress up, so there was no point in quarrelling about it.

The only consolation out of all this, the Earl thought, was that he need not attend the Ball.

Then it suddenly struck him that if he did not, everybody would be aware, though there had been no public announcement, that he had been thrown over by Heloise.

It would prove what they had all suspected was true.

When Heloise had insisted that their engagement should be kept secret, the Earl while slightly mystified, had agreed.

It had never occurred to him that she might be hoping for a better offer, at the same time ensuring that she did not lose face.

He had thought the reason was that they were making sure in their own minds that their love was something that would last forever.

Then it would be the perfect love that all men and women had sought since the beginning of time.

The Earl was now remembering how careful Heloise had been not to let the gossips talk about them.

'I *want* it known!' he had protested at a Ball two nights before.

This was when she had said after their second dance that she would not give him a third.

'People will talk,' she said in a whisper.

'Let them!' the Earl replied. 'I want to dance with you, my darling, I want to hold you close to me.'

'That is something you must not do,' Heloise said quickly. 'You know people are watching us. How can they not do so when you are so handsome?'

She looked up at him alluringly as she spoke.

He made the obvious reply:

'And you are too beautiful for any man's peace of mind. I want to kiss you, Heloise, you know that.'

'Later, much later,' she whispered. 'Not here, at any rate.'

He told himself she was being sensible.

After all, before their engagement was

announced, he would have to speak to Lord Penbrook, and tell his Grandmother.

His other relations would also be upset if they were 'kept in the dark.'

'Let us wait just a little longer,' Heloise pleaded when he discussed it with her. 'I love you, you know I love you, Ingram. But after all, you had a great many love-affairs before you met me.'

'They meant nothing—absolutely nothing,' the Earl said firmly, 'compared to what I feel about you. And you are more beautiful than anyone I have ever seen!'

Heloise had smiled, taking such praise as her due.

Almost every man she met said the same thing.

She was well aware, because of her red hair and green eyes, that she shone amongst the other girls of her age.

They all looked very English with their fair hair, blue eyes, and pink-and-white complexions.

Fortunately Lord Penbrook was well off.

Heloise could afford to dress in a way that accentuated not only her colouring, but the movements of her supple body.

No-one knew how long she had practised in front of a mirror until she could walk with a Siren-like movement of her slim figure.

She made it impossible for any man in the room not to watch her.

Every movement of her hands, the way she held her head, and the flicker of her eye-lashes had been practised to perfection.

The result was sensational.

Where she and the Earl were concerned, naturally people guessed there was something between them.

It struck the Earl now that it would cause a sensation if he did not appear at the Devonshire House Ball.

If he did, on the other hand, and was not accompanied, every person in the Ball-Room would be talking about it.

'What the Devil shall I do?' he asked himself.

He was intelligent enough to be aware that a large number of men would be delighted to learn he had been 'turned down.'

They would consider that it 'served him right' for being too successful, too rich, and too good-looking!

Of course they were jealous of him. How could they not be?

Also the Mothers who had given up aspirations for their daughters to become the Countess of Ardwick would resume the chase.

'What am I to do?' the Earl asked himself again.

Deep in his thoughts, he suddenly became aware that his horses had come to a standstill.

He looked out of the window.

They were in a narrow street and ahead of them there had been an accident.

14

It was something that was happening frequently in London these days because of an increase in the population.

Many of the streets were too narrow for the amount of traffic now surging through them.

The Earl could hear men were shouting noisily at each other.

As he looked out, he could see that the wheels of two vehicles were interlocked.

He opened the door and got out of his carriage.

The vehicles involved were a Post-Chaise and a Hackney-Carriage.

The drivers were yelling foul oaths at each other.

The Hackney-Carriage had partially collapsed onto one side.

The Earl walked along the pavement.

A number of small boys and some elderly women had gathered at the scene of the accident.

They moved to let him pass as if recognising he was someone in authority.

Standing just ahead, looking at the carriage, were those who had been the occupants of it.

They were, the Earl saw, a young girl and a small boy.

The latter was pulling out of the Hackney-Carriage a Spaniel who was obviously frightened by the collision.

The Earl walked up to the girl and said:

'May I be of any assistance? You seem to be

in trouble.'

She was small and slight, and she looked up at him as if in surprise that he was speaking to her.

As she did so, he realised that she was exceptionally pretty—in fact 'lovely' was the right word.

She was indeed very young and, he thought, unsophisticated and frightened.

'W-we ... have been ... in a ... collision,' she said unnecessarily. 'I ... I do not quite ... know what to d-do.'

'I am afraid,' the Earl remarked with a slight touch of laughter in his voice, 'you will not be able to proceed any further in that vehicle!'

'N-no ... I suppose ... not,' the girl replied.

The small boy now had the Spaniel in his arms. '*Bracken* is afraid, Lupita,' he said.

'I think he will be all right if you put him down on the ground, Jerry,' the girl answered, 'but keep hold of his lead.'

As she spoke, the two drivers were still shouting furiously at each other.

They were using language which was, the Earl thought, most unsuitable for the ears of a young girl.

The street they were in was a poor one.

Apart from the damaged Hackney-Carriage, the traffic consisted mostly of carts and wagons.

'What I suggest,' the Earl said, 'is that I give you and your little brother, as I suspect he is, a lift to wherever you are going.'

'That is ... very kind of you,' she said, 'but...'

'Have you any luggage?' the Earl interrupted.

'Yes ... we have.'

She pointed to a small trunk which was on the box of the Hackney-Carriage.

The Earl signalled to his footman, who was standing by the door of his carriage.

The man came running.

'Take that trunk down, James,' he said, pointing towards the Hackney-Carriage, 'and put it up behind us.'

'Very good, M'Lord.'

He got the trunk down which did not appear to be very heavy.

'Now suppose you get into my carriage,' the Earl said, 'while I try to get the two drivers to stop shouting at each other and clear the road so that we can proceed.'

The girl took the hand of the small boy.

They followed the footman, who was walking ahead with the luggage.

The Earl stepped out into the road.

In a few words he managed to silence the angry drivers.

They knew authority when they met it.

With sour faces they proceeded to move their horses and the battered vehicles so that the Earl's team could pass them.

It took a little time, but the Earl supervised

17

the operation until the road was clear.

He returned to his own carriage and got in.

The young girl was sitting on the back seat with the small boy and the dog opposite her.

As the Earl sat down, she said:

'It ... it is very kind of you ... and both my brother and I are ... very grateful.'

'It is a pleasure!' the Earl replied. 'Now, where do you want to go?'

His footman stood at the door of the carriage, waiting for instructions.

There was a little pause before she replied:

'I ... I wonder ... do you know of a ... quiet Hotel where ... we could ... st-stay?'

The Earl looked at her in astonishment.

'A Hotel?' he asked. 'But surely, if you have come to London you have relatives or friends with whom you are going to stay?'

'N-no ... I am ... afraid not,' the girl answered. 'Jerry and I just want ... somewhere very ... quiet and respectable ... where no-one will ... f-find us.'

The Earl was intrigued.

There was nothing he liked more than a mystery, or a puzzle that needed untangling.

There was obviously something strange about these two young people.

Turning to the footman, he said:

'Home, James!'

The footman shut the door.

As the horses began to move off, the Earl said:

'I think the first thing we should do is to introduce ourselves. I am the Earl of Ardwick.'

The girl opposite him gave a little gasp.

'I have heard of ... you!' she exclaimed. 'You have very fine race-horses ... and you ... won the Gold Cup at Ascot ... last year.'

The Earl smiled.

'I did indeed, but I am surprised that you should be aware of it.'

'My F-Father was very ... interested in racing,' the girl replied, 'and when his ... sight began to fail I ... I used to ... read to him about the race-meetings in the ... newspapers.'

She spoke without any affectation.

It made the Earl feel sure that she was a country-girl.

She obviously knew very little about London.

A quiet family Hotel she was envisaging for herself and her brother would be difficult to find.

The Proprietors would also think it strange that a young girl was travelling without a chaperon.

'You have not yet told me who you are,' the Earl prompted.

'I am Lupita Lang ... and this is my brother, Jeremy, whom we have always called "Jerry."'

She hesitated for a moment before she went on:

'Perhaps I should also ... tell you that he is the Earl of Langwood.'

19

The Earl looked at her in astonishment. Then he repeated:

'The Earl of Langwood! In which case I knew your Father, who I imagine must now be dead.'

'H-he ... died last ... winter,' Lupita replied.

There was a note in her voice which told the Earl how much it upset her.

'I am deeply sorry to hear that,' the Earl said. 'I met your Father two years ago at Newmarket, and I am sure I saw him at Ascot last year, when, as you say, I won the Gold Cup.'

'Y-yes ... he was there,' Lupita agreed, 'but ... now that he is ... d-dead ... Jerry and I have ... had to run away.'

The Earl looked at her.

'Run away?' he queried. 'Why, and from whom?'

There was a pause when he wondered if she was going to tell him the truth.

At that moment there was the sound of a bang, and Jerry moved quickly to the open window.

Outside, red-coated soldiers were marching down the road led by their Band.

It was a sight with which Londoners were now very familiar since Queen Victoria's Diamond Jubilee two weeks before.

But to Jerry it was new and exciting.

He leaned out of the window as far as he could to see the soldiers marching past.

It was then that Lupita said in a low voice that only the Earl could hear:

'Th-there is ... somebody trying to ... kill Jerry!'

CHAPTER TWO

The Earl stared at her in astonishment.

Then, when he would have spoken, she put her finger to her lips.

He was aware that she could not speak in front of the small boy.

As they drove on, the Earl said:

'I think, Lady Lupita, it would be a great mistake for you to stay at a Hotel alone with Jerry. As I knew your Father, I feel in a way responsible for you, and I therefore suggest that you stay at my house in Grosvenor Square.'

Lupita looked at him in surprise.

'St-stay with you? But we ... have only just ... met ... you.'

'I know that,' the Earl answered with a smile, 'but you perhaps do not understand the difficulties you would encounter in a strange Hotel. Also, owing to the Queen's Jubilee, every Hotel in London is heavily booked.'

'I ... I did not think of ... that,' Lupita said, as if it were very careless of her.

'Then let me suggest that you stay with me,' the Earl went on, 'at least until you can get in touch with your relatives. You will be amply chaperoned, as my Grandmother is with me at the moment.'

He paused to smile at her before he

continued:

'She is getting on for eighty, but it would never have occurred to her to miss the Jubilee celebrations, and she intends to enjoy every moment of it!'

'Thank you … thank you very … much!' Lupita said. 'It is very … very … kind of you … and I know if Papa were alive, he would be … extremely grateful.'

The Earl did not say any more, but he was wondering what all this was about.

Despite his anger at the way Heloise had behaved, he was now finding himself interested and intrigued.

How could anyone as attractive as the girl sitting beside him be running away?

And not from a man who was pursuing her, but who was intent on killing her brother.

He thought it must be her imagination and could not be true.

At the same time, because he had known and respected the Earl of Langwood, he was determined to get to the bottom of the problem.

It did not take long to reach the large house which the Earl owned in Grosvenor Square.

The horses drew up outside it and James jumped down.

The Earl was then aware the footman was holding the gown-box.

In it was the fancy-dress which Heloise had intended wearing at the Duchess of

24

Devonshire's Ball.

He vaguely wondered, since she was now going with the Duke of Dunbridge, what she had chosen instead.

Then he told himself she was utterly despicable and he would not think of her.

The front-door was opened the moment the horses drew up outside it.

The footman went ahead to put the gown-box inside.

The Earl helped Lupita out of the carriage and Jerry followed them, leading his dog.

As in all the Earl's houses, the hall at Grosvenor Square was extremely impressive.

It had a magnificent crystal and gold staircase, and a huge chandelier which glittered in the light coming from the high windows.

The Earl gave his hat and gloves to a footman.

The Butler hurried ahead to open the door of a room at the end of the hall.

As they entered, Lupita thought it was the most attractive room she had ever seen.

The Earl was walking across to where a lady with white hair was sitting by the mantelpiece.

Because it was July, there was no fire in the grate.

Instead, the fireplace was filled with flowers whose vivid blossoms made a glorious patch of colour.

'You are back already, Ingram?' his Grandmother exclaimed. 'I was not expecting you so early!'

'I have brought you some visitors, Grandmama,' the Earl replied, bending down to kiss her cheek. 'This is Lady Lupita Lang, and her brother, who is now the Earl of Langwood. I dare say you will remember the late Earl.'

'Langwood!' the Dowager Countess exclaimed. 'Of course I remember him. A very handsome man.'

She turned towards Lupita.

'Your Mother, my dear, was very beautiful, and I can see you are very like her.'

Lupita dropped a curtsy.

'It is kind of you to say so, and I am so glad that you knew Papa.'

'Lady Lupita and Jerry are staying with me,' the Earl explained, 'and I will go and make arrangements about their rooms.'

He left the Drawing-Room, and the Dowager Countess said to Lupita:

'Sit down, my dear, and tell me about your Father. I am so sorry to hear that he is dead.'

'I ... I miss him ... very much,' Lupita answered. 'Jerry and I live in the country, and we came to London quite ... unexpectedly.'

'I am delighted that you should stay here with my grandson,' the Dowager Countess said.

Jerry, who was playing with his dog, looked up.

'If there is a garden here,' he said, 'may I take

Bracken in it?'

'I am sure you can,' the Dowager Countess said as she smiled.

She picked up a small silver bell which was on a table by her side and rang it.

The door was at once opened by the Butler, and the Dowager Countess said:

'This little boy wants to take his dog into the garden, Dawkins. I am sure you can send one of the footmen with him.'

'Yes, of course, M'Lady,' the Butler replied. He held out his hand to Jerry, who jumped up, saying:

'We were in the Hackney-Carriage for a long time. I do not think *Bracken* will like being in London.'

'I expects he'll soon get used to it,' Dawkins replied.

They were still talking as they left the room, and the Dowager Countess said:

'Tell me, dear child, about your Mother. I remember seeing her in several Ball-Rooms before she married your Father and thinking how extremely beautiful she was.'

'Mama died three years ago,' Lupita answered, 'and ... my Father missed her so much ... that I do not think he minded ... dying. He ... caught a very bad cold before Christmas ... I blame myself for not ... looking after him better ... as Mama had always done.'

'So now you are looking after your little

27

brother,' the Dowager Countess said.

'Yes,' Lupita agreed.

'I am sure he is very lucky to have you.'

The Dowager Countess glanced up at the clock.

'I hope you will understand, my dear, if I now go and lie down before dinner. Otherwise I will feel too tired to come downstairs.'

She got to her feet as she spoke and walked across the room.

Lupita hurried to open the door for her, and as she did so the Earl was coming in.

'You are going upstairs now, Grandmama?' he asked.

'You have guests, and I know that you are going to the Ball,' the Dowager Countess replied. 'So I am going to lie down, otherwise this charming young lady will be having dinner alone.'

'As it happens, Grandmama, I shall be here,' the Earl said.

His Grandmother looked at him in surprise.

'I understood you to say that you were dining with the Marlboroughs.'

There was a slight pause before the Earl said:

'My plans have been changed, and I shall be dining here, Grandmama.'

The Dowager Countess did not ask any questions, and merely walked towards the stairs.

Her lady's-maid was waiting to help her up to her room.

As she went, the Earl was thinking quickly.

He was certain that Heloise would not miss the dinner-party, which was being given by the Duke and Duchess of Marlborough.

Instead of going there with him as arranged, she would be going with the Duke.

That, he thought, was a further humiliation which he had no intention of suffering.

He was still undecided as to whether he would go to the Ball or stay at home.

Either way, he knew it would cause a great deal of gossip which would certainly not be to his advantage.

He was suddenly aware that Lupita's luggage had been taken in the carriage round to the side-door.

The gown-box which the footman had handed in was still lying in the hall.

It was then he had an idea.

He walked into the room where he knew Lupita was waiting.

She was standing by the window, waiting to see her brother go into the garden with his dog.

The sun was shining on her hair.

Without thinking she had pulled off her hat when she was alone, just as she would have done at home in the country.

Her hair was, the Earl thought, different from anything he had seen on another woman.

It was fair, but so pale that it seemed in the sunlight almost silver.

And yet it appeared to glitter as if it had a life

29

of its own.

She turned to look at him as he came into the room.

He was aware at that moment that she was the most beautiful girl he had ever seen.

She was not spectacular like Heloise.

But she had, with her fair hair and her blue eyes, a spiritual beauty that was something seldom if ever seen in the Social World.

As the Earl walked towards her he thought she might have stepped out of a Story-Book, or, rather, from a medieval painting depicting an Angel, or even the Madonna Herself.

The Earl reached her and said quietly:

'Now that we are alone, we can talk. So will you tell me what you meant when you said in the carriage that someone is trying to kill your brother?'

Lupita looked away from him as if she were shy.

He was aware that her profile was perfect.

She had a small, straight nose and features that might have been sculpted by an Ancient Greek.

She was obviously thinking, and after a moment's pause the Earl said:

'Please tell me the truth, the whole truth, and I will try to help you.'

She glanced at him quickly before she said:

'I ... I must not ... impose on your ... kindness ... but I *am* frightened ... and I do not ... know what to do.'

'Then tell me what is frightening you,' the Earl said. 'I promise that I am very good at solving conundrums, however difficult they appear to be.'

'I am sure that is ... true,' Lupita said, 'but ... you may think I am ... imagining all this.'

'Let me be the judge of that,' the Earl replied.

Because she was irresolute, he took her by the arm and led her to a sofa, where they sat down.

'Now, begin at the beginning,' the Earl prompted. 'When your Father died, what happened?'

'It ... happened quite suddenly ... and ... naturally I was ... very upset ... and because the weather was so bad ... only a few of our relations came to the ... Funeral Service. But they all wrote to me saying ... how s-sorry they were.'

'And you did not think of suggesting that you might live with any of them?'

'I had no wish to leave home, and I have to look after the Estate which now, of course, is Jerry's.'

'Your Father had no other children?' the Earl asked.

'I ... I had a brother who was born two years after I was, but he died when he was only eight.'

The Earl thought that must have been a blow to Lupita's Father.

He could understand that he would desperately want to have another son.

As if she followed his thoughts, Lupita said:

'Papa adored Jerry ... and although he was so ... young, he was already teaching him how he must look after other people we employ, carry on the improvements he was ... making, and, of course, keep up his racing-stable.'

'So that is what you have been trying to do,' the Earl commented. 'But surely you have someone to chaperon you?'

Lupita smiled.

'We have Jerry's Governess with us, who is a very sweet woman. She taught me before I went to School. At the moment she has had to go to look after one of her sisters who is ill, but she is coming back at the end of the month.'

'And so you were alone,' the Earl said, trying to get a picture in his mind of the situation.

'We were ... alone,' Lupita said, 'until our ... Cousin Rufus Lang ... appeared.'

'And who is he?' the Earl asked.

'He is the son of Papa's younger brother ... and has always ... lived in ... London.'

'I think I have heard of him,' the Earl remarked. 'I believe he is a member of White's Club.'

'He is very smart ... and goes ... he tells me ... to all the ... best parties and knows ... everybody of ... importance.'

There was a pause, and the Earl said:

'Go on.'

'You will ... understand,' Lupita said, hesitating, 'that ... if Jerry had not been born

32

'... Rufus would ... have come into the ... title.'

The Earl raised his eye-brows.

'Surely you are not suggesting that it is Rufus who has attempted to kill your brother?'

'I knew ... you would ... not believe ... me,' Lupita murmured, 'but ... two or three ... things happened ... and that is why I ... came away.'

'Tell me about them,' the Earl encouraged her.

He spoke in a way which he knew most women found beguiling.

Lupita looked up at him.

He thought her large blue eyes, pleading with him to understand, were very moving.

'The first thing which ... upset me,' she said in a very low voice, 'happened ... a week ago.'

'What happened?' the Earl asked.

'My Father always said we were ... never to go up on ... the Tower of the house ... because it was ... dangerous. The roof is very old ... and some of the crenellations are ... crumbling.'

'I suppose Jerry disobeyed your Father's orders,' the Earl said.

'I missed him when he should have been playing in the Sitting-Room with his dog, and I wondered where he was.'

Lupita looked up at the Earl again to see that he was listening before she went on:

'I ... I could not find him ... until I saw that the door up to the Tower was open ... and I

33

heard voices.'

'So you went up to find out what was going on,' the Earl said.

She nodded.

'Just as I ... reached the top ... I heard Cousin Rufus say to ... Jerry:

'"Lean over a little further and see if you can see right down to the ground below us. There may be a rabbit hiding there."'

'Was there likely to be a rabbit?' the Earl asked.

'No ... of course not ... rabbits never come as near to the house ... as that,' Lupita answered.

'And I suppose Jerry was obeying him,' the Earl suggested.

'He was just about to do so when Rufus saw me. He had been bending towards Jerry and I was almost certain his hand was stretching out ... as if to push him!'

'Do you really think he would have pushed the little boy over?' the Earl asked.

'I could not believe it myself,' Lupita answered, 'but I thought Rufus looked as if he were frustrated when I appeared.'

'What did you do about it?' the Earl asked.

'I said to Jerry, "Come away from there at once, Jerry! You know Papa never allowed us to come up here!"'

'What did Jerry say to that?' the Earl prompted.

'He said, "Cousin Rufus wanted to see the

34

roof, but I did warn him to be very, very careful."'

Lupita gave a deep sigh before she went on:

'I said, "What you are doing is very dangerous. Come down at once!"'

'So you took Jerry to safety. What did your Cousin say?'

'It was later that evening when he said: "I am sorry if I made a mistake by going up on the roof, but I was particularly eager to see the view which your Father always told me was very fine from the top of the house."'

'But you did not believe him?'

'Of course not,' Lupita answered. 'Papa had always said that no-one must ever go up onto the roof. After that ... I took the ... key away.'

'That was sensible of you,' the Earl agreed. 'Then what else happened?'

'You ... will not ... believe me,' Lupita said, 'but ever since I have been small I have ... somehow been able to ... read people's ... thoughts. After that, whenever I saw Cousin Rufus ... looking at Jerry ... I knew he was ... thinking that if ... only he were not there, the Estate would be his ... and he ... would be the ... Earl of Langwood.'

There was a little sob in Lupita's voice as she spoke the last words.

Then, as if she were afraid of losing her self-control, she went on quickly:

'But ... something ... else happened which ... made me ... run away.'

35

'What was that?' the Earl asked.

'Yesterday, when I came back to the house from riding with Jerry, there was no sign of Cousin Rufus.'

'He did not ride with you?' the Earl asked.

'N-no. Although I ... suggested it, he said he wanted to ... stay behind.'

'Then when you returned he was not in the house?'

'I did not ... know where he was ... but when I went up to my room to change I ... looked out of ... the window.'

'What did you see?' the Earl enquired.

'We have a lake in front of the house which is very deep and has shifting sand at the bottom of it, which is why Jerry and I have never ... learned to ... swim.'

'What did you see on the lake?' the Earl asked.

'We have a rowing-boat, which is seldom used now that Papa is dead. He used to take us in it and we would row down the stream, then back again.'

The Earl thought that sounded harmless enough, but he waited, and after a moment Lupita continued:

'To my surprise ... from my bedroom window ... I could see Cousin Rufus ... standing in the boat where it was ... tied up ... then bending ... down.'

'What was he doing?' the Earl asked.

'I was not ... sure,' Lupita answered, 'but I

36

thought it was ... very strange ... so when he came back to the house ... I waited until dinnertime ... then I asked:

'"Can you swim, Cousin Rufus," and he replied:

'"Extremely well, as it happens."

'My Governess, Miss Graham, was interested, and he told her how he had won a Championship prize in Switzerland and had also competed in swimming races in Germany.'

'So you thought that he was looking at the boat so that he could use it while he was swimming,' the Earl said. 'How does that have anything to do with your brother?'

'Because I was ... suspicious,' Lupita answered, 'I got up very early this ... morning before even the servants were ... awake, and went down to ... look at the boat. Something kept ... telling me that was what I ... should do ... and I had been ... unable to sleep because I was ... so worried.'

'What did you find?' the Earl asked.

'I found that there was a hole in the boat that had been ... plugged with what Papa once told me was a kind of ... black sugar which dissolves if it is very long ... in the water.'

The Earl was suddenly still.

'I do not believe it!'

'It is ... true,' Lupita said, 'and as I am sure you know ... when the sugar ... finally dissolves, the boat would ... fill with water and ... s-sink.'

37

'So you think your Cousin was going to suggest taking Jerry out rowing on the lake, and then when the boat started to sink he would swim to safety, while your brother would be drowned!'

Because it seemed so extraordinary, the Earl was working it out for himself.

'I expect ... I would have been ... asked to go ... too,' Lupita replied.

The Earl did not speak, and after a moment she said:

'Please believe ... me! I know it ... sounds incredible ... but every nerve in ... my body tells me that Jerry is ... in danger!'

The Earl put out his hand and laid it over hers.

'I do believe you,' he said. 'Now tell me how you got away.'

'I woke Jerry as soon as I got back to the house and told the servants to order our fastest carriage, which is drawn by two horses.'

Lupita paused for breath before she went on:

'I ... I packed a few things and the servants carried the trunk ... into the yard so that we would not be ... seen by Cousin Rufus, if he was ... awake, leaving by the ... front-door.'

'But he did not see you?' the Earl asked.

'He does not get up early for breakfast because he drinks so much wine at night,' Lupita explained, 'and I knew that by the time he was called we must be ... far away ... from him.'

38

'And how far did you go?' the Earl enquired.

'We drove in our own carriage until the horses were too tired to go any further. Then I took a Post-Chaise at a Posting-Inn and when we reached London I hired a Hackney-Carriage in which we had that accident.'

'This is the most extraordinary story I have ever heard!' the Earl exclaimed. 'But you did the right thing, and I can only commend you, Lady Lupita, for being extremely intelligent and brave in the way you are trying to protect your young brother.'

'Then you ... really believe ... me?' she asked.

He saw the relief come into her face like radiance.

He thought it made her even lovelier than she was already.

'What do you intend to do now?' he asked. 'You can hardly run away from your Cousin for ever.'

'I ... I shall be ... all right as soon as I can find some relatives who will come and stay with us. Perhaps they will be ... strong enough to make Cousin Rufus be ... aware that he is not ... welcome.'

'Now that you have told me your troubles,' the Earl said, 'I have an idea to put to you which I think will be of advantage to us both.'

'You know I would be ... very happy to do ... something for you when ... you have been so ... kind to us,' Lupita said.

'What I am going to suggest,' the Earl answered slowly, 'is that tonight you attend with me a Ball being given by the Duchess of Devonshire.'

He saw the astonishment in Lupita's face.

'I have ... read in the ... newspapers about the Ball that is being given in honour of the Queen's Diamond Jubilee,' Lupita said, 'but ... how could I possibly ... go to ... it?'

'Very easily,' the Earl replied, 'because I have a gown for you, and you will come as my partner.'

'I ... I cannot ... believe it!' Lupita exclaimed. 'But I ... do not ... understand how ... that will ... help you.'

'It will help me,' the Earl replied, 'because the partner with whom I was going is now unable to do so.'

He chose his words carefully, having no intention of telling Lupita the truth.

'So you would ... like me to accompany ... you instead?' she asked. 'But ... suppose I do not ... look right and you are ... ashamed of me?'

The Earl smiled.

'That is very unlikely. I assure you, you will look very lovely in a gown which I know will fit you.'

He thought as he spoke that the fancy-dress which he knew was a confection of jewels and floating panels of chiffon, would fit almost anyone.

Lupita clasped her hands together.

'I have ... never been to ... a Ball. When I was eighteen ... at the end of last year ... Papa was going to bring me to London ... but then he ... died.'

She drew a deep breath before she added:

'To go to ... the Devonshire House Ball of *all* Balls! I cannot ... believe it!'

'Nevertheless, that is what we will do,' the Earl said. 'Now, I suggest that, like my Grandmother, you go and rest before dinner so that you will not be too tired to dance with me when we reach the Ball-Room.'

Lupita laughed, and it was a very pretty sound.

'How could I be ... tired when I am ... going to a Ball? I am sure I shall ... wake up to find this is ... all a ... dream!'

'You will wake up and find yourself at Devonshire House, dancing with me!' the Earl assured her. 'Perhaps I should mention that you will be dressed as Cleopatra, and as I expect you know, she was very beautiful!'

'Oh ... I do hope I do not ... disappoint you!'

Lupita spoke sincerely.

The Earl was aware that no other woman of his acquaintance, including Heloise, would ever believe they could be a disappointment to him with their looks.

'I am quite sure you will grace Devonshire House,' he said confidently. 'In fact, we both

41

will!'

Lupita laughed as if he had said something funny.

Then she jumped up from the sofa.

'I will go to lie down,' she said, 'because I could not bear to be sleepy and miss one moment of being at the most important Ball of the whole Diamond Jubilee ... celebrations!'

'I see you have been reading the Society Columns in the newspapers very carefully,' the Earl smiled.

'I read about the Jubilee celebrations because they ... sounded so exciting, but I never ... thought for a ... minute that I ... should ever have ... a part in ... them!'

'Now you are going to play a very important part,' the Earl said, 'so go upstairs, shut your eyes, and do not dare to wake up until I send my Housekeeper to call you!'

Lupita laughed again before she ran across the room to obey his orders.

Only as she reached the door did she look back to say:

'Thank you ... thank you! You have waved a magical wand and now ... like "Cinderella" ... I really believe that I am ... going to ... the Ball!'

'I promise you that is what you are doing,' the Earl replied.

As Lupita disappeared, he told himself he had been very clever.

He had an answer for the gossips, and also

42

he would, he hoped, annoy Heloise.

She always disliked competition.

He had the feeling that with Lupita wearing the jewelled dress which had cost him so much money, Heloise would be put in the shade.

CHAPTER THREE

As soon as Lupita had gone upstairs, the Earl went into action.

He had been noted when he was in the Army for his powers of organisation.

He was aware that this talent was something he needed specially at this moment.

First of all, he had sent for his Housekeeper, Mrs Fielding, who had been at the house since he was a boy.

He told her exactly what he wanted as regards Lupita.

Then he said:

'See that the small boy, His Lordship, is properly looked after and that the housemaids or the footmen play with him and keep him amused.'

'I'll do that, M'Lord,' the Housekeeper answered.

'The one thing he must not do is to disturb his sister. Do you understand?'

'I'll do me best, M'Lord,' the Housekeeper promised.

The Earl then sat down and wrote a letter to the Duchess of Devonshire.

As it happened, she was his Godmother, and was very fond of him.

As the Duchess of Manchester she had been an enchanting beauty.

The Marquess of Hartington, who afterwards became the Duke of Devonshire, was her lover for many years before they could be married.

Now she had grown old and rather fat, but she had a charm that was irresistible.

She was also very fond of good-looking men, especially her Godson.

The Earl knew she would be intrigued by his letter, and she would certainly allow him to do what he planned.

He sent the letter off by a groom to Devonshire House, then wrote another to be taken to the Egyptian Embassy.

By this time it was getting late, and he knew it would soon be time for him to change for dinner.

The Cook had, of course, been alerted that His Lordship was dining in, and the Earl had ordered dinner much later than usual.

The guests had been invited to arrive at Devonshire House at ten-thirty.

But the Earl was well aware that huge dinner-parties like the Duchess of Marlborough's, which were being given before the Ball, would take far longer than the dinner he was sharing with his Grandmother and Lupita.

To make it easier for both of them, he told the Housekeeper that Lupita was to wear an ordinary gown at dinner.

He wanted her to change into her fancy-dress afterwards.

'Of course,' he said, 'have her hair done, and I think she will need some jewellery from the safe.'

He had assumed that while Heloise had sent him back the gown in which she was to impersonate Cleopatra, she would have kept the expensive pearl earrings he had bought for her.

Having made enquiries, he learnt this was true, and it made him even more angry than he was already.

He had been unfailingly successful all his life in everything he undertook.

He still could hardly credit that Heloise had deceived him into thinking that she really loved him.

Now she was going to humiliate him in front of all his friends.

Those who knew the Earl well would have been warned that he was in a fighting mood.

The look in his eyes and the hardness of his lips showed that he was now fighting a new battle which he was determined to win.

It was something he had invariably achieved in the past, and it had earned him a medal for gallantry of which he was extremely proud.

That he had survived several dangerous campaigns which had killed his brother-Officers was entirely due to his intelligence and to his exceptional powers of leadership.

Now he knew that he was fighting a battle

for his pride and his self-respect.

It was another he was determined to win.

*   *   *

When Lupita came down to dinner she was in a simple white gown that she had worn at home when she dined with her Father.

She had packed in a hurry to get away from her home and had thrown in anything that came to hand.

She had known it would be disastrous if Cousin Rufus had realised they were leaving.

All she could think of was that she must take Jerry to safety.

She had made up her mind that they would be safer if they were lost in London, rather than anywhere else.

When she went into Jerry's room to say goodnight to him before she went down to dinner, she found that he was sitting up in bed.

He had some toys which the Housekeeper had found for him.

'Look what I have got, Lupita,' he said when she appeared.

'A train, a Teddy Bear, and a Golliwog,' Lupita exclaimed. 'You *are* lucky!'

'And there will be more toys for me to have tomorrow,' Jerry said with satisfaction.

Mrs Fielding, who was with him, explained:

'We put all His Lordship's toys up in the attics, M'Lady, and I promised your brother

48

I'd bring some more down and put them in the *Boudoir*, which His Lordship says you're to have as your Sitting-Room.'

'That is wonderful!' Lupita exclaimed. 'How kind His Lordship is to think of it!'

She put her arms round Jerry and said:

'Goodnight, darling. Go to sleep soon, because you have had a long day.'

'*Bracken* says he likes it here,' Jerry answered. 'There's quite a big garden, Lupita, and he had a 'normous supper!'

'As I expect you did too,' Lupita laughed.

She kissed her brother lovingly.

When she left the room he was once again playing with his toys.

She sent up a little prayer of thankfulness.

How different it would have been if they had stayed alone in some Hotel.

What was more, now that she thought of it, they might have made a fuss about having Jerry's dog.

'We have ... been lucky ... so ... very lucky,' she told herself as she went downstairs.

The Earl put himself out at dinner to be amusing, both to his Grandmother and to Lupita.

He told them stories of when he was the same age as Jerry and, because Lupita was interested, talked about his race-horses.

The food was delicious.

Time seemed to slip by so quickly that Lupita could hardly believe it when the Earl said:

'Now you must go and get dressed. I want to leave in about half-an-hour.'

'I am sure I shall . . . not be . . . ready!' Lupita exclaimed.

'I am coming to your room in ten minutes,' the Earl said, 'to make sure that you are, and that you are dressed exactly as I want you to be.'

She gave a little cry of horror and ran from the Dining-Room and up the stairs.

Mrs Fielding was waiting with the Seamstress, who, Lupita learned, lived in the house.

When they helped her into the dress, she thought it was the most exciting and elaborate costume she could imagine.

It was too long, however, and also too big in the waist.

The Seamstress was taking in the waist when the Earl knocked on the door and came in.

He saw at a glance that Lupita was going to look exactly as he wanted her to.

He had remembered, because he was very well read, that Cleopatra was not of Egyptian blood but Macedonian.

She was in direct descent from the Macedonian Ptolemy Soter, founder of the dynasty which had ruled Egypt for nearly three hundred years since the death of Alexander the Great.

According to the History books, her skin

was 'as white as milk, her eyes as blue as the Aegean, and her hair was burnished gold.'

It had occurred to him that he could stage a more striking and dramatic entrance for Lupita if he came, not as Mark Antony, but as Julius Caesar.

Caesar had arrived in Egypt in pursuit of his defeated rival, Pompey the Great, and had a love-affair with Cleopatra seven years before Mark Antony even met her.

He had therefore told the Duchess in his letter that he was coming as Julius Caesar.

'I shall be accompanied,' he wrote, 'by a new "Cleopatra," who is the daughter of the late Earl of Langwood.'

He had the idea that the Duchess and the late Earl had been friends many years earlier.

He was sure he was right in thinking that Lupita's Father had been a great admirer of the beautiful Duchess of Manchester.

As the Earl now came into the bedroom, Lupita looked at him apprehensively.

He was dressed not as Heloise had intended as the dashing Mark Antony, but as Julius Caesar.

The costume was the same, but on his head the Earl wore a laurel wreath, characteristic of Julius Caesar as a victorious general.

He had also added a touch of white powder to his dark hair.

He was, however, not so much concerned with his own looks as with Lupita's.

When she met Julius Caesar, Cleopatra was not yet twenty-one.

She was young, untouched by any man, and had the beauty and purity of a young girl.

Heloise had chosen the gown to make herself look seductive and, as she had said, 'as if it expressed all the legends and magic of Egypt.'

However, to the Earl's satisfaction, it looked entirely different on Lupita.

He prided himself on knowing how to make a woman look her most beautiful.

It was just as he prided himself on being able to decorate his houses more strikingly and in better taste than anyone else could.

He was aware that apart from the enveloping headdress that was portrayed in every portrait of Cleopatra, Heloise had intended to wear her long red hair flowing over her shoulders.

It might not be historically correct, but it would certainly have become her.

The Earl had instead instructed Mrs Fielding that Lupita's hair was to be arranged close to her head and must hardly show at all.

What was then displayed was her long neck, which made her look very young and vulnerable.

The dress, with its jewelled breastplates, was festooned all over the bodice with semi-precious jewels.

Below the waist it flowed out in loose panels of chiffon which floated as she moved.

One glance told the Earl that they were too long, and he ordered the Seamstress to cut them so that they just touched the floor.

He also realised that while the dress fitted closely, it did not accentuate the curves of Lupita's body as it would have done on Heloise.

But it contrived, as the headdress did, to make her seem very young and breathtakingly beautiful.

On his instructions the Seamstress added a frill of chiffon over the shoulders.

As she was doing so, the Earl's Secretary came in, carrying a tray.

On it were some of the Ardwick jewels which his Mother had worn on important occasions.

When not in use, they were kept in a closely guarded safe.

The Earl picked up from the tray a necklace consisting of two rows of perfect Oriental pearls which had just a touch of pink in them.

They had always been admired when his Mother wore them.

As he fastened them round Lupita's neck, she gave a little gasp.

He put a broad diamond bracelet round each of her wrists.

Then he chose two magnificent diamond earrings that sparkled like stars in her ears.

The Earl was thinking how often Heloise had hinted that she longed to wear the Ardwick jewels.

But he had not agreed to her doing so until they were officially engaged.

For one thing, the most outstanding of the jewels were easily recognisable to the Social World.

Secondly, he had vowed to himself that no-one would wear the Ardwick jewels except the woman he married.

Now he cast this resolution aside.

Tonight he was determined that Lupita should eclipse Heloise.

He hoped to teach her a lesson she would never forget.

He stood back to look at Lupita.

'I have … never seen … anything so … so lovely!' Lupita said in an awed voice as she looked at the diamond bracelets on her wrists.

The Earl was certain that was what people would be saying about *her*.

However, he left it to Mrs Fielding and the housemaids to exclaim over and over again how marvellous Her Ladyship looked.

He glanced at the clock on the mantelpiece.

'I think we should leave,' he said, 'but first you must show yourself to my Grandmother. She is waiting downstairs specially to see you.'

'But of course!' Lupita cried excitedly.

She did not wait for the Earl, but ran out of the room.

The Earl smiled at Mrs Fielding.

'You have done a splendid job,' he said.

'It wasn't difficult, M'Lord,' Mrs Fielding

replied. 'Her Ladyship's the most beautiful young lady I've ever seen, an' so sweet it's a real pleasure to do anything for her.'

The Earl followed Lupita.

He found her in the Drawing-Room, twirling round and round in front of his Grandmother to show her how the chiffon panels swung out.

She had sandals on her feet, also sparkling with jewels.

Although they were a trifle too big, she knew she would be able to dance in them.

The Dowager Countess looked up at her grandson and said:

'If you do not look more distinguished than anyone else in the Ball-Room, I shall be exceedingly disappointed!'

'I have a feeling, Grandmama,' the Earl replied, 'that you will be proud of both of us! I wish you were coming with us.'

'As I told the Duchess,' the Dowager Countess said, 'I am too old for Balls.'

The Earl thought that in fact she was wise.

She had attended a dinner-party last night and had had luncheon today at Buckingham Palace with the Queen.

However, as he kissed her goodnight, he said again:

'I wish you were coming too, Grandmama, but we will tell you all about it tomorrow and not miss out a single detail.'

'That is what I shall be waiting to hear,' the

Dowager Countess replied, 'and Bless you both! You look absolutely marvellous!'

It was what the Earl thought himself.

Lupita, when she looked in the mirror, could hardly believe that the glittering image she saw was not really the reincarnation of Cleopatra.

The carriage was waiting outside.

The Butler put a cape of Russian sables over Lupita's shoulders.

The horses started off.

As they did so, Lupita slipped her hand into the Earl's.

'I am so excited!' she said. 'I am half afraid the carriage will break down or something will prevent me at the last moment from reaching the Ball.'

She spoke like an excited child.

The Earl knew there was nothing flirtatious in the way she had slipped her hand into his.

It was done in the same way as she would have impulsively taken the hand of her brother or her Father.

'Now, listen to me very carefully,' he said, 'because I am going to tell you what we will do when we get there.'

*   *   *

The Earl had deliberately waited until he thought most of the guests, including the Marlborough House party, would have arrived at Devonshire House.

56

He was therefore not surprised when they entered the hall to see only a short queue of guests mounting the staircase to be greeted by the Duke and Duchess.

A Blue Hungarian Band was playing as he and Lupita moved slowly upwards.

There was a Master of Ceremonies dressed in Elizabethan costume to ask their names and which characters they represented.

Then, when they reached the top of the staircase, in a stentorian voice he announced them to the Duke and Duchess:

'The Earl of Ardwick and Lady Lupita Lang, representing the most noble Gaius Julius Caesar, Dictator of Rome, and Her Majesty Queen Cleopatra of Egypt.'

The Duchess of Devonshire's eyes were twinkling as she said to Lupita:

'I am delighted to meet you, Lady Lupita. Your Father, as I expect you know, was an old and dear friend of mine.'

Lupita curtsied as she said:

'Thank you very ... very ... very ... much for allowing me to come to your ... wonderful Ball!'

The Earl then led her towards the Ball-Room, which was massed with orchids, lilies, and other exotic plants.

They had been brought, the Earl was aware, from the conservatory at Chatsworth, the Duke's great country house in Derbyshire.

Footmen in eighteenth-century livery were

handing round champagne.

Having reached the door, the Earl did not take Lupita into the Ball-Room.

Instead, he drew her along a side passage and into an empty Sitting-Room.

He went to the open door.

He thought it was unlikely that the Marlborough House party, after a formal dinner, would arrive before at least another half-hour.

A footman came hurrying up to him.

''Er Grace asked Oi to tell Yer, M'Lord, that 'er's just being carried into th' Ball-Room.'

'Thank you,' the Earl replied.

He had learned that the Duchess of Devonshire was representing Zenobia, Queen of Palmyra.

She had arranged, after receiving her guests, to be carried into the Ball-Room in a palanquin on the shoulders of six bearers.

The Duke was dressed as the Emperor Charles V and had no intention of doing anything so theatrical.

He was a shy, retiring man by nature, but he adored his wife and was content to let her do anything she wished.

As the Duchess was getting into the palanquin, four Egyptians presented themselves to the Earl in the Sitting-Room.

They had come in answer to the letter he had sent to the Egyptian Embassy.

They were dressed as slaves, although he

doubted if their costumes were exactly authentic.

However, they looked the part and had brought what he required, which was a long, narrow board.

The Duke had had the brilliant idea that Lupita should enact the romantic story of how Cleopatra had got herself smuggled into Julius Caesar's presence rolled up in a carpet.

The Egyptians set the board down on the floor.

Obediently, because the Earl had told her in the carriage what he wanted her to do, Lupita lay down on it.

Then she was wrapped up, not in a carpet which would have been too heavy, but in a bed-spread which had a Persian design on it.

It would appear to those who glanced at it exactly like an Oriental carpet.

The Earl waited until the Duchess had been carried into the Ball-Room.

She was greeted with cheers and claps from the large number of people already assembled there.

He had noticed as he passed the doorway that all the Dowagers had seated themselves round the walls.

There were also some fantastically dressed young men standing in the background, waiting for the dancing to begin.

These were the men the Earl knew would be the first to query why he was not with Heloise.

They would undoubtedly be consumed with curiosity as well as being 'bowled over' by the beauty of Lupita.

As the applause that greeted the Duchess subsided, the Earl gave a signal.

The four Egyptians raised the board on which Lupita was lying and placed it on their shoulders.

The Earl had been wise enough to ask for men who had been in the Army.

They could be relied upon to march in unison with each other and to carry their burden with an expertise he would not have expected of an ordinary civilian.

The Earl walked in, followed by the Egyptians.

As they set the board down on the floor of the Ball-Room, the Master of Ceremonies announced once again:

'The most noble Gaius Julius Caesar, Dictator of Rome!'

Lupita was completely covered by the Persian bed-spread.

For a moment everyone looked bewildered.

The Egyptians then ceremoniously removed the coverlet and the Earl moved forward to help Lupita to her feet.

The light from the huge chandeliers glittered on the jewellery on her headdress and on her gown.

She seemed to shimmer with a thousand lights as if she were a star.

'Her Majesty, Queen Cleopatra of Egypt,' announced the Master of Ceremonies.

There was a moment of silence from sheer astonishment.

This was followed by everybody applauding and cheering with delight.

It was a complete and absolute success.

The Earl bowed and Lupita curtsied.

Then tongues began to wag as people started asking who she was and why they had not seen her before.

The Band started to play and the Earl put his arm round Lupita.

'Was it as you ... hoped?' she asked in a whisper.

'You were perfect!' he replied.

'And now I am at my very first Ball,' Lupita breathed with a rapt note in her voice, 'but I feel as if I am ... dancing on ... a cloud!'

She looked so radiant as she spoke that the Earl thought it was not surprising that everybody in the Ball-Room was looking at her.

They danced the first dance together.

Immediately many of the Earl's friends insisted on being introduced to Lupita, but he managed soon to be dancing with her again.

Meanwhile, the Earl had caught sight of Heloise.

He knew there was another reason she had wanted to come with the Duke.

She was wearing the Dunbridge diamonds,

61

which were famous.

Lionel Bridge, who was to be the first Earl of Dunbridge, was soldiering in India at the end of the last century with Sir Arthur Wellesley.

In one of his campaigns he had saved the life of the Nizam of Hyderabad.

The Nizam, naturally, had been extremely grateful.

As he possessed a private Diamond Mine of his own, he had given the young Officer an enormous number of uncut diamonds to take back with him to England.

The story had fascinated the Prince of Wales, who later became the Prince Regent, then King George IV.

It was whispered that some of the diamonds had paid a large number of His Royal Highness's outstanding debts.

A little later Lionel Bridge distinguished himself both in the Peninsula War and then at the Battle of Waterloo.

Eventually, whatever the pretext, he was rewarded by becoming the first Duke of Dunbridge.

He had certainly been a strange and unusual character.

When he was over forty he married a girl who was the daughter of another Duke and their wedding was the talk of the whole country.

The Duke had emulated King George IV.

Some people said he had even borrowed part

of the very spectacular clothes His Majesty had worn at his Coronation.

He had been described as looking 'like some gorgeous bird of the East.'

Tonight the 4th Duke had come dressed as his ancestor, with a train of crimson velvet inset with golden stars.

His large hat, Spanish in design, was decorated with ostrich feathers.

If the Duke looked fantastic, Heloise had been determined to outshine him and everybody else in the Ball-Room.

She was wearing an enormous tiara which was almost like a crown, glittering with the Nizam's diamonds.

Round her neck were ten strings of large diamonds reaching nearly to her waist.

She had several bracelets on each arm and huge earrings with diamond drops that almost touched her shoulders.

Her gown was, the Earl thought, very like the actual wedding-gown worn by the first Duchess.

On Heloise it was not particularly becoming, but there were yards of it trailing behind her.

In fact, it aroused little interest compared to the diamonds she was wearing.

The Earl, to his great satisfaction, learnt later that she had received some applause, but not nearly as much as Lupita had.

He had already heard several men making rude remarks about Dunbridge's hat.

He too was staring at it when Mrs Asquith, wearing the costume of an Oriental snake-charmer, came to his side to say:

'What is going on, Ingram? I thought you were coming with Heloise Brook.'

Margot Asquith was noted as being one of the most dangerous gossips in the whole of London Society.

The Earl, therefore, hesitated before he replied.

Then, before he could do so, she looked at Lupita and remarked:

'But of course, seeing who you are with, I understand! She is exquisite—quite exquisite!'

The Earl suddenly had an idea, and bending towards Mrs Asquith, he said almost in a whisper:

'Please be careful not to say anything about us yet. It is too soon, and we have not had a chance to talk to our families.'

Margot Asquith's eyes lit up.

There was nothing she enjoyed more than hearing of an engagement or an *affaire-de-coeur* before anybody else was aware of it.

'But, of course, dear boy,' she said. 'I will be very discreet.'

She patted the Earl on the arm and moved away.

He knew that not for one moment would she be able to keep the information to herself.

She would be telling everyone in the room that the Earl of Ardwick was not engaged to

Heloise Brook, as they had all expected.

In fact, his new love was Lady Lupita Lang!

Without even looking, the Earl was aware that the Dowagers were glancing towards him and beginning to gossip.

Taking Lupita by the arm, he drew her from the Ball-Room into the garden.

Here there were Chinese lanterns hanging from the trees and the paths were outlined with fairy-lights.

Lupita was too young and unsophisticated to realise that to be alone in the garden with a man was an indiscretion.

No strict Mama would have allowed her *débutante* daughter to leave the Ball-Room.

The Earl made sure that Lupita could be seen from the windows as he pointed out to her some of the other guests.

Lupita was thrilled to see the Prince of Wales in the full glory of the Grand Prior of the Order of St John of Jerusalem.

They both laughed at the Countess of Westmorland who, as Hebe, had a huge stuffed eagle on her shoulder.

She found it impossible to cope with it when she was dancing.

But the most amusing was undoubtedly an American, Mrs Rowlands, who was representing Euterpe, the Muse of Music.

To Lupita's astonishment, she had electric lights woven into her hair so that they lit up the lyre she carried.

There were so many strangely garbed and exciting people to see, and Lupita was thrilled by them all.

The Earl too found himself enjoying the spectacle and forgetting for the moment how furious he was with Heloise.

Later, when he heard people criticising her display of diamonds as being 'somewhat vulgar,' he thought it served her right.

He was, however, aware that because Lupita was so lovely, they were not as surprised by his not being with Heloise as he might have anticipated.

He was determined to show Heloise he was not upset at her decision to marry the Duke.

He danced almost every dance with Lupita and made her refuse the invitations she received from other men.

This in itself fanned Margot Asquith's assertion that they were secretly engaged.

He was not surprised, when they said goodnight, that many of the older Dowagers to whom he spoke murmured:

'Congratulations, my dear boy!'

It was three o'clock in the morning when he eventually said goodnight to his hostess.

As he kissed her, the Duchess said:

'You know, Ingram, that I am seething with curiosity, and if you do not tell me what is going on, I will never speak to you again!'

'You know I could not bear that to happen, so expect me sometime in the afternoon.'

'And do not dare to forget that appointment!' the Duchess said, wagging her finger at him.

The Earl and Lupita waited in the hall while their carriage was being brought round to the front-door.

She admired the huge marble basin which was filled with water-lilies.

She looked rather like a lily herself, the Earl thought as she touched the white blooms with the tips of her fingers.

Then, as they got into the carriage and the horses moved off, Lupita said:

'It was wonderful ... wonderful ... wonderful! I can never thank you enough for taking me to such a ... marvellous party! I shall remember it for the rest of my life!'

'I am quite certain that after tonight you will be invited to a great number of others,' the Earl replied.

She looked at him in surprise.

'But ... why should people invite me?'

'You have been a great success, Lupita,' he said, 'and as many of the guests will have known your Father, you will by now have been added to their lists and, as I have said, the invitations will flood in.'

'I ... I cannot believe ... it!' Lupita said.

Then she gave a little cry.

'If that happens, Cousin Rufus will know ... where I am!'

'You are not to worry about him,' the Earl

said. 'I will deal with your Cousin so that he does not upset you again.'

There was silence for a moment before Lupita said:

'But ... I am sure ... absolutely sure ... that he will ... still want to k-kill Jerry. I do not think I told you that his Valet ... whom he brought with him when he came to Wood Hall, told our servants that his Master was heavily in debt ... and that he was glad to ... escape from London as the ... Duns ... were threatening him.'

It was what he might have expected, the Earl thought.

It would undoubtedly make Rufus Lang determined by one means or another to get hold of the money which now belonged to a small boy of six.

It was only this child who stood between him and the title and all that appertained to it.

As they drove on, the Earl was thinking that he must not make the mistake of underestimating the menace Rufus Lang incorporated.

He was undeniably a serious danger to the young, unspoilt, and very beautiful girl sitting beside him.

CHAPTER FOUR

Lupita awoke as the maid was pulling back the curtains.

She then brought in a breakfast-tray and put it down beside the bed.

'Breakfast in bed?' Lupita exclaimed. 'That is very luxurious!'

''Is Lordship's orders,' the maid said, 'an' as 'e'd like t'take you driving in th' Park, 'e asks if you'll be downstairs by eleven-thirty.'

'Of course I will!' Lupita exclaimed.

She glanced at the clock beside her bed and was amazed to see that it was just after ten.

'I am certainly quickly getting used to London ways,' she thought.

She was still eating her breakfast when Jerry came running into the room.

'Lupita!' he cried. 'They would not let me come in before 'cause they said you were asleep. You are lazy to sleep so long!'

'I was very late last night, dancing at the Ball,' Lupita said.

Jerry was not interested.

'I've got some new toys,' he said, 'and you must come and see them.'

'I will do so as soon as I get up,' Lupita promised.

Jerry walked round her room, looking at various things.

69

She knew he was really longing to go back to his toys.

She thought only the Earl could be so clever.

He not only had a garden in which *Bracken* could go when he wanted to, he also had been thoughtful enough to instruct the Housekeeper to get down for Jerry from the attic any toys she had hoarded there.

'I am lucky ... so very ... lucky,' Lupita told herself.

She thought of all the compliments she had received last night from the men who had danced with her.

In fact, there were not many besides the Earl, but other men had gone up to him, saying:

'I insist on being introduced to the most beautiful Cleopatra I have ever imagined.'

'It was really the dress, not me,' Lupita told herself.

At the same time, the thought that she had been a success was very exciting.

She hoped the Earl was pleased with her.

Mrs Fielding came to arrange her bath and help her dress.

Lupita put on the best day-gown she had brought with her and her prettiest hat.

She could not help feeling that after last night the Earl would expect her to look more spectacular.

When she went downstairs, he looked at her appraisingly.

He obviously did not feel that she looked so

70

countrified that he would change his mind and not take her driving.

Outside stood an elegant Chaise drawn by two perfectly matched horses.

The groom was sitting up behind, wearing a smart livery with a cockade in his tall hat.

Before they left the house the Earl gave instructions that one of the footmen was to keep Jerry occupied.

He suggested he would perhaps enjoy a ball game with the racquets which were in the Games Room.

As they drove on, Lupita said:

'You think of everything! How can you be so excessively kind and at the same time so ... clever?'

'Now you are flattering me,' the Earl answered. 'I am delighted to hear it, but actually it is I who should be paying you compliments.'

Lupita looked at him anxiously:

'I ... I was ... afraid,' she said in a small voice, 'that you would not think me ... smart enough to come driving with you.'

'I think you look charming,' the Earl replied. 'But I have constituted myself as your Guardian now that your Father is dead, so I have sent for a Bond Street Dressmaker to visit you this afternoon and provide you with the gowns you will need if you are to accept half the invitations that will be flooding in.'

To his surprise, Lupita laughed.

'I do not ... believe your story about the ... invitations,' she said.

'Just wait and see, and you will soon realise I am right,' the Earl replied.

He drove his horses with an expertise which she knew would have pleased her Father.

When they turned into Rotten Row, Lupita was certain their carriage looked far smarter than any other.

There were a great many exquisitely dressed Ladies sitting in open Victorias, holding up little sunshades.

There were also a number of Gentlemen on horseback who all seemed to know the Earl.

They drove slowly.

The Earl suddenly because aware that seated in an open carriage, with the Duke of Dunbridge beside her, was Heloise.

He drove past, knowing that she was watching him.

He, therefore, deliberately turned his head the other way to acknowledge the greetings of a man on horseback.

He thought with satisfaction how much it would annoy Heloise that everyone in sight was looking at Lupita.

They would certainly have recognised her as the Cleopatra of last night, and, he suspected, were now telling each other that they were secretly engaged.

He knew the fact that he was driving alone in Rotten Row with Lupita would confirm the rumour.

They would assume this because she was without a chaperon.

He had, he thought with satisfaction, skilfully 'passed Heloise at the winning-post.'

Although she was sitting on the back seat of the open carriage with Dunbridge beside her, opposite them was seated an elderly woman.

She was obviously playing the part of a chaperon.

It would be from four days to a week, the Earl calculated, before Heloise would be able to announce her engagement officially.

In the meantime, she would be told by everyone that the Earl of Ardwick was secretly engaged to the very beautiful girl beside him in his carriage.

As he drove on, he thought he had struck her a very effective blow.

It was something for which Heloise would never forgive him.

They drove in the Park for about an hour.

Then they went back for luncheon, at which the Dowager Countess joined them.

She wanted to hear everything that had happened last night.

The Earl told her how he had played the part of Julius Caesar and Lupita had been carried in wrapped in what looked like the carpet of the original story.

His Grandmother clapped her hands.

'Only you, Ingram, could have thought of

73

anything so original,' she said. 'I am sure it will be the talk of Mayfair for a long time.'

'That is exactly what I hope,' the Earl answered.

After luncheon, when they went into the Drawing-Room, he said he had some letters to write.

Then he had promised to call on the Duchess of Devonshire.

'Give her my love,' his Grandmother said, 'and tell her that I hope to see her tomorrow and hear her version of what happened at the Ball.'

The Earl smiled.

'I am sure that will take her a very long time.'

He walked towards the door, and as he reached it he turned back to say:

'You will not forget, Lupita, that the Dressmakers are coming this afternoon? Put on one side anything that takes your fancy, and when I come back I will decide if your choice is right or wrong.'

'I . . . I certainly could not decide anything by myself,' Lupita said. 'Supposing I make a terrible mistake and you . . . disapprove of . . . something I have . . . chosen?'

'I have told you, put them aside for me to see when I return,' the Earl replied. 'In fact, I am staying only a short time at Devonshire House, and I will be back long before you have finished decking yourself out.'

He left before she could say any more.

Lupita looked helplessly at the Dowager Countess and said in a low voice:

'I ... I feel, Ma'am, that I ... ought not to allow His Lordship to ... buy me clothes. At the same time ... I do not want him to be ... ashamed of me.'

'I am sure he could never be that, my dear,' the Dowager Countess smiled. 'My grandson has already told me that, as your Father and Mother are dead, he feels he must look after you and your brother. Just let him have his own way, and I am sure everything will turn out for the best.'

The way she spoke made Lupita think that the Earl must have confided in her.

After a moment she said in a low voice:

'D-did your ... grandson tell you ... why we had to ... run away?'

'He told me,' the Dowager Countess answered, 'and I am horrified that any man who is supposed to be a Gentleman should behave in such an appalling manner.'

She stopped speaking a moment, and then went on:

'Unfortunately when a great deal of money is at stake, it can often make people behave outrageously when one least expects it.'

She spoke sharply, and after a pause Lupita said:

'I ... I feel we are ... imposing on His ... Lordship ... but ... I was so ... frightened and did not ... know what to do.'

'What you must do is simply to let my grandson look after you,' the Dowager Countess assured her. 'He is very clever and very reliable, and I am sure you will never regret having turned to him for help.'

Lupita smiled.

'Thank you. You have made me feel much ... happier,' she said, 'because I have lived only in the country ... I am so afraid of doing ... something ... wrong.'

'Just enjoy yourself,' the Dowager Countess advised her.

When Lupita was told that the Dressmakers had arrived, she turned impulsively to the Dowager Countess.

'Please,' she begged, 'come with me. You always look so ... beautiful and have such ... exquisite taste, and I am so afraid of making a mistake.'

'Of course I will come if you want me to,' the Dowager Countess said. 'Now hurry up to your bedroom, where the Dressmakers will be waiting for you ... I will join you in a few minutes.'

Lupita did as she was told.

When she had gone the Dowager Countess sent up a little prayer of thankfulness that this attractive, unspoilt child had diverted her grandson's attention from Heloise Brook.

She had never liked that young woman.

Although she was very beautiful, the Dowager Countess realised she was conceited and concerned only with what she could get out of life.

Heloise Brook was not at all the sort of wife she had envisaged for her grandson.

Then, as if by a miracle, at the last moment, when she was sure Heloise was going to accept him, he had been saved.

She did not believe it possible that he could care for anyone so unsophisticated as the child he had taken under his wing.

At the same time, the Dowager Countess was aware she was saving him from being publicly recognised as a discarded Suitor.

'Everything is working out for the best,' she thought as she went slowly up the stairs, 'and the longer Ingram is interested in these young people, the better!'

The gowns which had been brought from Bond Street were all, Lupita thought, so fascinating that she was bewildered as to how to choose between them.

It was the Dowager Countess who decided that the best way to do things was to start at the beginning with morning-gowns.

They then selected several for the afternoon, and finally reached those for the evening.

Each one that was held up for their approval, Lupita thought, seemed more exquisite than the last.

She always turned to the Dowager Countess to see her reaction before she asked the Saleswoman to set any on one side.

Finally, after a great deal of discussion, they chose three gowns for the morning, three for the afternoon, and four for the evening.

'I am sure I shall not need all these!' Lupita exclaimed.

'I am quite certain that in two or three weeks' time you will be saying that you have nothing to wear!' the Dowager Countess replied.

The Saleswoman agreed.

'You look lovely in every one of them, M'Lady,' she said to Lupita, 'and I'm not exaggerating when I say that I've not had anyone as beautiful as Your Ladyship to dress for years!'

'I cannot believe that,' Lupita protested, 'but it is so kind of you to say so.'

She was blushing a little as she spoke, and the Dowager Countess thought it was very touching.

When they had finished, the Dowager Countess retired to the *Boudoir* which opened out from her bedroom.

She said she had some letters to write.

Lupita ran downstairs, wondering how soon the Earl would be back.

The Saleswoman had arranged with Mrs Fielding to leave the gowns 'On approval' until His Lordship had seen them.

She added that she was quite sure he would approve of everything they had chosen.

When Lupita reached the hall, Dawkins, the Butler, came towards her with a silver salver in his hand.

'A number of letters have arrived for you, M'Lady,' he said, 'but I didn't like to interrupt until you'd finished with your visitors.'

'Letters ... for me!' Lupita exclaimed. 'Who can they be from?'

Dawkins smiled.

'I thinks, M'Lady, you'll find they're invitations.'

Lupita remembered what the Earl had said.

But she could not believe that the pile of letters on the silver salver were really invitations for her.

She took them from Dawkins and went into the Drawing-Room.

When she opened the envelopes she found he was right.

They were invitations for Balls and dinner-parties, all from distinguished people who she supposed must be friends of the Earl.

'He was right,' Lupita told herself, 'and I shall certainly need all the gowns I have chosen.'

She was reading the invitations again when the door of the Drawing-Room opened.

One of the footmen announced:

'The Honourable Heloise Brook, M'Lady!'

Lupita looked up in surprise.

Standing just inside the door was an exquisitely beautiful woman.

Lupita remembered she had seen her at the Ball wearing an amazing diamond tiara.

79

She had also been covered in more jewels than Lupita could imagine, even on a Queen.

She rose as Heloise moved sinuously across the room towards her.

She thought the newcomer was overwhelmingly lovely.

However, there was an obviously hostile expression on her face.

Looking at her in a very disdainful manner, Heloise said:

'I saw you last night, arriving at the Ball in a very strange manner. I cannot imagine how anyone who calls herself a "Lady" could disport herself in such a vulgar fashion!'

She seemed almost to spit the words at Lupita, who stared at her in astonishment.

She moved back a step or two as if afraid Heloise might even strike her.

'I ... I was with the ... Earl of Ardwick,' she said hesitatingly.

'I am well aware of that!' Heloise snapped. 'He obviously picked you up from nowhere and brought you to the Ball merely to insult and humiliate me!'

'I ... I do not ... understand,' Lupita stammered.

'You should have been aware that the way you were behaving with the Earl was outrageous, and extremely unladylike. I cannot understand how your parents could have allowed it.'

'M-my parents are ... d-dead.'

'I suppose you thought you were clever clinging onto the Earl and making a spectacle of yourself which has all Mayfair laughing.'

Lupita could not think of what to say.

She could only stare at this beautiful woman, aware of how angry she was but not understanding why.

'I suppose you realise,' Heloise went on, 'that the Earl is in love with me and wanted me to become his wife. The only reason he put on that ridiculous charade was to tell me how bitterly he misses me.'

She paused for a moment before she said:

'And if you think you can ingratiate yourself into his affections, you are very much mistaken! He loves me! Can you get that into your stupid head? I know he will never love anyone else in the same way.'

Her voice rose almost to a shriek.

Then she looked Lupita up and down in what was an extremely offensive manner before she added:

'Go back where you belong and realise that "Country Bumpkins" who make themselves a laughing-stock are very much out of place in well-bred London Society.'

With that she turned and walked out of the room.

Lupita sank down onto the rug in front of the fireplace and covered her face with her hands.

She had thought it was such fun last night

when the Earl had told her what he wanted her to do.

She had loved every minute of being dressed in the beautiful costume as Cleopatra and driving with him to the Ball.

It had all seemed like stepping into a Fairy Tale.

She had been carried into the Ball-Room and came out from under the carpet just as Cleopatra had done.

It had never occurred to her that she was doing anything wrong, or, as this beautiful woman had said, 'vulgar.'

Now she thought that perhaps her Father and Mother would not have approved of the part she had played, even in a private house.

'I ... must go ... home,' she thought.

Then she knew she could not do that because of Jerry.

She felt the tears come into her eyes.

Then, as they blinded her, the door opened.

She thought it was one of the servants, who would go away again.

The door shut and she heard footsteps coming towards her.

She tried to wipe away the tears with the back of her hand, but they kept running down her cheeks.

As someone stopped behind her, she knew it was the Earl.

'What has happened?' he asked. 'I heard that Heloise Brook has been here. Has she upset you?'

It was impossible for Lupita to reply.

Then, to her astonishment, the Earl picked her up in his arms and carried her to the sofa.

He saw the tears running down her cheeks and took a handkerchief from his pocket and put it into her hand.

'Now tell me why you are unhappy,' he said. 'When I left you, you were laughing and enjoying all the things we were doing.'

There was silence as Lupita tried to wipe away her tears.

Then, as she knew the Earl was waiting, she said in a broken little voice:

'The ... the beautiful Lady who ... came here said I was ... vulgar ... and that everyone was ... laughing at me for the way I ... behaved last night.'

The Earl made a sound, but Lupita was not certain what it meant, and she went on:

'She told me to ... g-go back to the ... country, where I came from ... but how can I ... I do that while Cousin ... Rufus is ... there?'

She sounded so unhappy that the Earl put his arm around her.

Instinctively she turned to hide her face against his shoulder.

'She ... she said,' Lupita sobbed, 'that I was making a ... laughing-stock of you.'

The Earl's arms tightened.

'What she really means,' he said, 'is that *I* was making a laughing-stock of *her*!'

He spoke almost to himself.

Then he said quietly:

'Now, listen to me, Lupita, and perhaps I should have told you this before.'

He knew she was listening and went on:

'I thought Heloise Brook was very beautiful, and for the first time in my life I considered being married and settling down in the country.'

'She is ... she is ... very beautiful,' Lupita murmured.

'Then I learned,' the Earl said, 'that her beauty is only "skin deep." Underneath she is scheming, and all she wants in life is an important title—not love!'

Because she was so surprised, Lupita raised her face from his shoulder to look up at him.

Her eye-lashes were wet and there were still some tears left on her cheeks.

Yet, looking at her, the Earl thought she was infinitely more beautiful than Heloise had ever been.

At the same time, he felt an urge to protect her and prevent her from ever being unhappy.

'What made me angry,' he said quietly, 'was that I was fool enough to be taken in by her beauty.'

He paused a moment, then he went on:

'I did not realise that underneath she was scheming to marry the highest title possible, while at the same time keeping me dangling on a hook in case the Duke of Dunbridge did not propose to her!'

'I ... I find that ... difficult to believe,' Lupita said. 'H-how could she ... not want to ... marry you?'

The Earl knew it was an innocent question, and he said gently:

'Some women, Lupita, want sparkling diamonds more than they want a throbbing heart.'

'But ... if she is going to marry a ... Duke ... why was she so angry with ... me?'

'I am quite certain your Father would have thought it a great joke,' the Earl replied, 'and it was no more vulgar than our hostess who, if you remember, entered the Ball-Room on a palanquin.'

Lupita gave a little sigh of relief.

'Yes ... of course,' she said, 'and ... everybody clapped her.'

'Just as they clapped us,' the Earl said.

He looked at his handkerchief, which Lupita was holding on her lap.

He took it and very gently wiped away her remaining tears.

'There is nothing to cry about,' he said, 'and I want you to look as happy and as beautiful as you looked last night.'

He looked down at the invitations that were scattered on the floor, and said with a smile:

'You see, I was right! I knew you would have a great number of invitations, and I am sure there will be a great many more arriving tomorrow.'

There was a little pause before Lupita said:

'You are ... quite certain that I can ... go to them? People will not be ... saying I am all those ... horrid things that ... Lady said I was?'

'People have been saying that you are as beautiful as your Mother, whom they remember,' the Earl said, 'and they are not surprised that your Father, who was outstandingly handsome, should have such a lovely daughter.'

Lupita blushed. Then she said:

'You are just saying that to make me feel better! But I must not ... hurt you in any way ... and perhaps Cousin Rufus will have ... left by now ... and Jerry and I can ... go back to the country.'

'You are—thinking of me?' the Earl asked.

'Of course I am. How could I do anything else when you have been so wonderfully kind to us both?'

There was an expression in the Earl's eyes that had never been there before as he looked at her.

He realised she was being entirely sincere, and he said quietly:

'I think we will enjoy a few more days in London, then next weekend you and Jerry shall go back to your home. But I am coming with you and my Grandmother will accompany us.'

'You mean ... you are both coming to ... Wood Hall?' Lupita asked.

'Of course, if, as I hope, you will invite us to come,' the Earl said. 'I want to see your home, and I assure you that your Cousin Rufus will behave properly if I am there. I will also make certain that when I leave, he goes too.'

Lupita gave a little gasp.

'That is the most wonderful thing you could possibly do,' she said. 'Oh, thank you, thank you! How can you be so kind? I know that if you sent Cousin Rufus away he would ... perhaps be too frightened to come back.'

'Leave all that to me,' the Earl said. 'Now I want you to smile and look pretty, and I suggest we go upstairs and look at the gowns that you have chosen.'

Lupita was smiling as she asked:

'Shall I put them on for you? If you are going to spend so much money, we should make quite certain they fit.'

The Earl laughed.

'Now you are being practical, and that is something I appreciate! Yes, of course, you go and put them on, one after the other. I will join Grandmama in her *Boudoir* and wait for you to come and show them to us.'

Lupita jumped to her feet.

'I will do that, and thank you for being so kind ... and understanding.'

She hesitated a moment. Then she said:

'You are quite ... quite certain that I am ...

not doing something that will … do you any harm?'

'Quite, quite certain!' the Earl said quietly.

CHAPTER FIVE

The young man with whom Lupita had been dancing took her, when the music stopped, into the Conservatory.

'I love flowers,' she said, 'and these are very beautiful.'

'You are like a flower yourself,' he said.

She gave him a shy little smile and bent forward to touch a rare orchid.

The Conservatory was exactly what she might have expected to find in a large house in Chelsea.

The Dowager Countess had told her before she went there that Lady Godwin was a great connoisseur of beautiful things.

Lupita was therefore enjoying not only the treasures in the house, but also the flowers.

She learnt that they had been brought from every part of the world.

The Dowager Countess had gone with the Earl and Lupita to the dinner preceding the dance, but had left soon afterwards.

'I am too old to stay out late,' she said, 'and I shall enjoy just watching for a few minutes you young people moving round the floor.'

The Ball-Room was an attractive one, although not as large as the one at Devonshire House.

It had long French windows opening out

into the garden.

The murals at one end of the room were scenes of Venice.

Everywhere Lupita looked she found something she wanted to study because it was so beautiful.

But she did not have the opportunity.

All the young men in the party wanted to dance with her, and so far she had had only one Waltz with the Earl.

As he had not been in the Ball-Room for some time, she guessed that he had gone to the Card-Room.

In fact, on the way from Grosvenor Square he had said:

'This is really a young people's party tonight, and if you do not see me on the Dance-Floor, you will know I am playing cards.'

She could not help feeling that she wanted to dance with him again and hoped he would soon reappear.

She moved up to another strange blossom she did not recognise and thought it must have come from the East.

It was then the young man said to her:

'You are very lovely, in fact the most lovely person I have ever seen. If I did not know you were engaged, I would ask you to marry me.'

Lupita turned to look at him in amazement.

'Engaged?' she said quickly. 'I am not engaged! What made you think that?'

The young man smiled.

'Everybody knows you are going to marry the Earl of Ardwick,' he said, 'and I think he is the luckiest man in the world!'

'But ... it is not ... true!' Lupita protested. 'The Earl is ... acting as my ... Guardian now that my Father is ... dead, but I assure you ... he has no ... intention of ... marrying me.'

She thought as she spoke of how bitter and angry the Earl's voice had been when he spoke of Heloise Brook.

It would take him a long time, Lupita thought, to get over the way she had behaved.

He might, in consequence, never marry.

The young man beside her took her hand in his.

'If what you are telling me is true,' he said, 'then perhaps I have a chance, and I can only tell you, Lupita, that I fell in love with you the moment I saw you.'

Lupita turned her head away.

'I ... I find that ... hard to believe,' she said, 'although it is ... true that my Father fell ... in love with my Mother ... before he had even ... spoken to her!'

'And that is what happened to me,' the young man said.

His name was Anthony Benson.

Lupita thought that while he was quite good-looking, he seemed young and impetuous, and not at all the type of man she wanted to marry.

She could not define to herself exactly what

91

she meant by that.

She just knew that even if Mr Benson were in love with her, she was sure she would never love him.

Because she did not want to seem unkind, she said:

'Of course ... I am very ... honoured that you ... should feel ... like that ... about me ... but we have ... only just ... met, and before I ... married I would ... have to be very ... very ... certain that I ... loved somebody and he ... loved ... me.'

'I do love you! I love you more than I can put into words!' Anthony Benson declared. 'And if, as you say, you are not secretly engaged to the Earl, then I shall go on asking you, Lupita, until you say yes.'

Lupita gave a little laugh.

'You may have to do that for years and years.'

'Then that is what I will do!' he said determinedly.

He came a little nearer to her, and she said quickly:

'I think we ... ought to go ... back to the ... Ball-Room. Someone ... might ... wonder where ... I am.'

'I want to take you into the garden and kiss you,' Anthony Benson said.

There was a determined look on his face that made Lupita feel frightened.

Before he could stop her, she moved quickly

towards the Conservatory door.

As she reached it, another couple came in to look at the flowers.

She slipped past them.

To her relief, as she reached the Ball-Room she saw the Earl standing in the doorway.

Because she could not help herself, she ran towards him and he said:

'Oh, there you are, Lupita. I was wondering what had happened to you.'

'I ... I have ... been in the ... Conservatory,' she said breathlessly. 'Please ... please ... dance with me!'

The Earl looked slightly surprised.

But as the music had started up, he put his arm around her and drew her onto the floor.

They danced a few steps before he asked:

'What has upset you?'

'I ... I cannot ... tell you here,' Lupita answered, 'but I would ... like to g-go home.'

'But of course,' the Earl agreed. 'It is nearly two o'clock, and you will need your "Beauty Sleep" if we are to repeat this performance every night!'

Lupita gave a little cry.

'Surely there is not ... another Ball ... tomorrow?'

'I expect so,' the Earl replied. 'I told you you would be a success, and this is the result!'

They finished the dance in silence.

As they went from the Ball-Room, Anthony Benson was waiting outside in the hall.

Lupita would have slipped past him, but he caught her hand.

'I will come and see you tomorrow,' he said. 'What time will you be alone?'

'I ... I do not ... know.'

'Then I shall sit on your doorstep until you let me in,' Anthony Benson said.

'Oh, please ... do not ... make any ... trouble for me,' Lupita begged.

'If anyone is in trouble, it is me!' he retorted. 'You know I want to see you, and you are being deliberately elusive. I must see you, Lupita!'

'I will have to ... ask the Earl what ... we are doing,' she answered. 'After all ... I am staying with him as ... his guest.'

'Everybody knows that!' Anthony Benson said in a somewhat hard voice.

He looked across the hall to where the Earl was waiting with an expression of impatience on his face.

'Are you really telling me the truth,' Anthony Benson asked, 'when you say you are not going to marry him?'

'Of course ... I am,' Lupita answered.

She twisted her hand from his and ran towards the Earl.

A footman was standing beside him with the fur cape which the Dowager Countess had lent her.

He put it over her shoulders, and without saying anything the Earl walked towards the front-door.

Outside, his closed carriage was waiting and Lupita got in.

When the footman shut the door and the horses started off, the Earl asked:

'Now, what is this all about and what was young Benson saying to you?'

'He ... he asked ... me to ... marry him,' Lupita answered.

There was a moment's silence. Then the Earl asked:

'And what did you reply?'

'I said that ... we had ... only just met ... and I would never ... marry anyone ... unless I ... loved him ... very much.'

'That was the right answer,' the Earl said. 'But I should tell you that young Benson's Father is a very distinguished man and extremely wealthy. You might do worse.'

Lupita turned her head to look at him in astonishment.

There was a candle-lantern burning opposite them in the carriage, and he saw the expression in her eyes.

Then she said in a very small voice:

'Are ... you really ... hoping I shall ... be married ... so that ... you will be ... free of me?'

'No, no, of course not,' the Earl said sharply. 'I never thought of such a thing.'

'Anthony Benson said that ... everybody thought I was ... engaged to you ... but I told him ... that was not ... true.'

The Earl felt a little guilty.

He had deliberately started the rumour in order to hurt Heloise.

Now for the first time it struck him that he might have harmed Lupita's prospects of finding a suitable husband.

As if she were trying to reason it out for herself, Lupita said:

'I ... I think perhaps ... Miss Brook might have spread the rumour ... because she ... accused me ... of trying to ... marry you.'

'And are you?' the Earl asked dryly.

Lupita gave a little laugh.

'I am ... sure that ... when you ... marry,' she said, 'it will be to ... somebody not only very ... very ... beautiful, but ... also very ... very ... important ... perhaps a Princess.'

'I think you are inventing stories about me,' the Earl said, 'and I have no intention of marrying anyone.'

Lupita thought this was what he was bound to say after the way Heloise had behaved.

She therefore answered:

'I can ... understand that you have been ... hurt, but please ... it must not ... spoil you ... or make you bitter and ... cynical.'

The Earl was so surprised at what she said that he could not think of any reply.

They drove on in silence until they were nearing Grosvenor Square.

Then he said as if he were thinking of her rather than himself:

'I expect young Benson will call on you tomorrow. If you do not want to see him, tell me, and I will give orders to the servants that you are not at home!'

'Perhaps ... that would be ... rather rude,' Lupita said.

'You cannot have it both ways,' the Earl answered. 'Either you are willing to see him, in which case he will undoubtedly go on asking you to marry him, or else you must make it clear that you are not interested in him.'

There was a note of irritation in his voice which Lupita did not understand.

It made her feel nervous, and she said quickly: 'Please ... can I ... think it over and perhaps ... talk to your Grandmother ... about it? I have ... never had a proposal of ... marriage before ... and I do not want to ... be unkind.'

'Like all women, you want to "have your cake and eat it"!' the Earl said.

As he spoke, the carriage came to a standstill outside the house.

Without waiting for a footman to open the door, he opened it himself and got out.

As Lupita followed him up the steps and into the hall, she thought he looked angry.

It frightened her, and she hurried up the stairs without saying goodnight.

She had the feeling, which she could not explain, that the evening had been disastrous.

When later she got into bed it was some time before she fell asleep.

*   *   *

The next morning her breakfast was brought to her as usual.

Jerry came rushing in to tell her with wild delight that *Bracken* had caught a rat in the garden.

'Cook is very pleased with *Bracken*,' he announced, 'and she has given him a very large bone for being such a clever dog!'

He climbed up onto Lupita's bed.

He told her exactly how *Bracken* had first smelt the rat in some rubbish, then finally caught it.

'It was a very big rat,' he said, 'and Henry said *Bracken* was very brave because it might have bitten him.'

Henry was one of the younger footmen who was looking after Jerry.

Lupita suspected that he enjoyed his time in the garden rather than having to be on duty in the hall.

Jerry was still talking when the maid came in to say:

''Is Lordship's compliments, M'Lady, but could yer be ready in 'alf-an-hour's time, 'cause 'e's taking you an 'Is Young Lordship t' th' Zoo.'

Before Lupita could reply, Jerry gave a whoop of excitement and jumped off the bed.

'I'll go and say we will be ready, Lupita!' he cried. 'Hurry! Hurry!'

He ran from the room.

As Lupita got up, she thought it was typical of the Earl to be so thoughtful.

She dressed in a quarter-of-an-hour and was just putting the finishing touches to her hair when a footman came to the door.

When the maid answered it he told her that there was someone downstairs wanting to see Her Ladyship.

'Who is it?' Lupita asked quickly, thinking, although it seemed incredible, that it might be Anthony Benson.

''Is name's Matthews,' the maid said, having consulted the footman. 'A Mr Matthews.'

Lupita gave a little cry.

She knew the man waiting to see her was the Farm Manager from Wood Hall.

'I will come at once,' she said, and added to the maid: 'Please bring my hat and bag downstairs.'

She did not wait for an answer, but followed the footman to a small room which opened off the hall.

It was one Lupita had not seen before.

Waiting there was Mr Matthews, an elderly man who had been her Father's Farm Manager for twenty years or more.

He was, she knew, thoroughly reliable and conscientious.

Holding out her hand to him, she said:

99

'This is a surprise, Mr Matthews. How did you find out where I was?'

'I had to find ye, M'Lady,' Mr Matthews replied, ''cause things be happening which I thinks you ought t'know about.'

'Then you knew I was here?' Lupita asked.

She was thinking that if Mr Matthews knew, then Rufus Lang would also be aware of where she was hiding.

''Twas th' wife,' Mr Matthews explained. 'She read 'bout you bein' at th' Duchess of Devonshire's Ball with th' Earl of Ardwick.'

Lupita gave a sigh.

She had forgotten in the excitement of going to the Ball that all the Court Circulars in the newspapers would give a description of such an important event.

Also they would give a list of the guests.

'We looked up the Earl of Ardwick's address in *Debrett's Peerage*, M'Lady,' Mr Matthews was saying, 'an' then I came up t'London.'

'By train?' Lupita asked.

Mr Matthews nodded.

'Tell me what has happened,' she begged.

She felt it must be something very serious, because Mr Matthews looked so solemn.

She knew he would not have left Wood Hall unless it was absolutely essential for him to do so.

Rather belatedly, she suggested:

'Suppose we sit down, and you tell me exactly why you have come.'

She sat down on the sofa and Mr Matthews sat in an armchair near her.

'Well, it's like this, M'Lady,' he began, 'I don't want to make trouble, but I can't believe your late Father would tolerate what Mr Rufus be doing.'

Lupita had a little throb of fear.

She might have guessed her Cousin Rufus was responsible for Mr Matthews' visit.

'Wh-what is he ... doing?' she asked in a frightened voice.

'First thing he did, M'Lady,' Mr Matthews answered, 'was to take away from me, protest though I might, all the money I'd drawn from th' Bank as I always do on Thursdays, to pay the wages, today being Friday.'

'He ... took the money from you?' Lupita repeated.

'That's right, M'Lady—every penny of it! And when I tells him I need it for the wages, he said his need were greater than theirs!'

Lupita wanted to say it was stealing, but bit back the words.

'Go on,' she prompted.

'I know also, because they tells me in the house, that he's been collecting together everything of value and laying it out on th' Billiard-table.'

Lupita looked at him in astonishment.

'Why would he do that?'

'I understands that he intends selling it all to someone who's coming down from London.'

101

'But ... it is not his to sell!' Lupita exclaimed.

'That's what I was thinking,' Mr Matthews agreed. 'And what's more, he ordered Mr Briggs to open the safe because he wants the jewellery that's kept there.'

Mr Briggs was the old Butler who had been at the Hall ever since Lupita could remember.

He guarded the safe as he would have guarded his life.

It not only contained all the silver, which was very old and valuable, but also her mother's jewellery.

There were also things like the tiara and the pearls that had been in the family for several generations.

'I hope Briggs did not give him the key!' she gasped.

'Mr Briggs was clever enough to say that Your Ladyship had taken it away with you,' Mr Matthews replied.

'That was clever of him,' Lupita said.

'But Mr Rufus,' the Farm Manager went on as if she had not spoken, 'threatens to blow off the lock!'

Lupita gave a cry of horror.

'I ... I do not believe it! We must stop him! We must stop him at once!'

'That's exactly what I thinks Your Ladyship would say,' Mr Matthews said with satisfaction, 'and when Mr Briggs tells me late last night what had happened, I caught the Milk Train at five o'clock this morn to come and find you.'

'I think you have been very, very clever,' Lupita said. 'Now, wait here while I go and find the Earl.'

She got up from the sofa, ran into the hall, and down the passage to the Study.

It was where she was sure she would find the Earl reading the morning newspapers and signing his letters.

He was there as she expected, sitting at his desk.

As she burst into the room, he looked up, then rose to his feet.

'What has happened?' he asked.

'Mr Matthews is here. He is our Farm Manager at Wood Hall, whom Papa trusted implicitly. He says terrible things are happening. Please ... please ... tell me what I must do.'

The Earl wasted no time asking questions.

He followed Lupita into the Morning-Room and shook hands with Mr Matthews.

He then listened attentively as the Farm Manager told his story all over again.

'You were quite right to come to Her Ladyship for help,' he said as Mr Matthews finished breathlessly, 'and she is fortunate to have anyone as sensible as you in charge.'

Lupita saw the Farm Manager beam with pleasure at his praise, but he merely said humbly:

'I tries to do what I think be right, M'Lord.'

'What I am going to suggest,' the Earl went on, 'is that you have something to eat and drink while I make preparations for us to leave for the country.'

Lupita looked at him in astonishment, but he continued:

'If we are to save the things that belong to your brother, no time must be lost. Tell Mrs Fielding to pack your clothes as quickly as possible while I make arrangements for the journey.'

The way he spoke told Lupita that she must do what she was told. So she ran upstairs.

She told Mrs Fielding and the maid who was still in her bedroom what they must do.

Then she went to find Jerry.

'I am sorry, darling,' she said, 'but we cannot go to the Zoo after all. We have to go home.'

'But I want to go to the Zoo,' Jerry protested. 'I want to see the bears and the elephants.'

'We will do so another day, I promise you,' Lupita said, 'but we must go home at once because Cousin Rufus is trying to steal away things that belong to you.'

'What's he stealing?' Jerry asked. 'Not my toys?'

'No, not your toys,' Lupita said, 'but money and treasures that belonged to Mama and Papa, and perhaps our horses.'

'He shan't have *Sambo*!' Jerry cried angrily. '*Sambo* is mine! I will not allow Cousin Rufus

104

to take him!'

'No, of course not,' Lupita said. 'That is why we have to go home and stop him!'

Sambo was a horse that Jerry had only just become big enough to ride.

He had been thrilled because Lupita had allowed him to have a horse.

Sambo was almost full size and very different from the small Shetland pony Jerry had ridden since he could walk.

Because her Father had taught Jerry, he was a very advanced rider for his years and admired by everyone on the Estate.

Sambo was almost black with a white star on his nose.

To Jerry he was a joy and delight.

Lupita had been worried when they had first run away that Jerry would miss *Sambo* unbearably.

Fortunately, with Mrs Fielding supplying him with so many toys, he had not been as distressed as she had feared.

Yesterday when she was playing with him he had said:

'If we are to stay here long, can *Sambo* come to London so that I can ride him in the Park?'

'We shall have to ask the Earl about that,' Lupita replied, 'but I think we will be going home soon. Anyway, I think *Sambo* would prefer to stay in the country.'

Jerry considered this for a moment before he said:

'But I want *Sambo* with me. I miss him!'

'I know you do, darling,' Lupita replied, 'but I am sure he is being well looked after, although I expect he is missing you too.'

She knew Jerry would soon forget his disappointment at not going to the Zoo when he knew he could see *Sambo* again.

To change the subject, she suggested he should take some of the toys he liked the best back home with him.

'Put them in a pile,' she said, 'for the maid to pack.'

Two hours later Lupita was told that they were driving to the station in twenty minutes.

The luggage was being taken downstairs by the footmen.

She quickly collected the light coat which matched her gown.

Having put on her hat, she was ready even before the carriage came round to the front-door.

The Earl was giving last-minute instructions to his Secretary.

These included, Lupita learned, cancelling his engagements for the next three or four days.

To her surprise, she then saw the Dowager Countess coming down the stairs.

She was dressed in a hat and a cloak and followed by her lady's-maid, carrying her jewel-case.

Before Lupita could ask the obvious question, the Earl said:

'Grandmama is coming with us, Lupita.'

'How wonderful!' she replied. 'But, surely, it will be too much for her?'

'She assures me she will enjoy it,' the Earl replied.

He walked towards the top of the stairs to greet his Grandmother.

'I hope you have everything you want, Grandmama,' he said, 'and you must forgive me for making you get ready in such a hurry.'

'It is something I got accustomed to when your Grandfather was alive, my dear,' the Dowager Countess said as she smiled, 'only usually he would say that we were off to Egypt or India without a thought as to what clothes I needed, or giving me time to buy them.'

The Earl laughed.

'At least we are not going as far as that,' he said, 'and Lupita is delighted that you are accompanying us.'

'I am over-whelmed at your doing so,' Lupita interposed, 'and it will be very exciting, Ma'am, to show you Wood Hall.'

'I am longing to see your home,' the Dowager Countess answered.

The Earl helped first his Grandmother into the carriage, then Lupita.

He and Jerry sat on the small seat with their backs to the horses.

The Earl's Valet and the Dowager Countess's lady's-maid followed in another carriage with the luggage.

They reached Paddington Station.

Here both Lupita and Jerry were thrilled to find that the Earl's private coach was attached to the train on which they were travelling.

It was commodious and comfortable, and the Drawing-Room had been decorated with crimson damask.

Jerry rushed about examining everything including the tiny Pantry where a Steward was preparing coffee for them.

He was enchanted with the two small bedrooms that opened out of the Drawing-Room.

It was the first private coach Lupita had ever seen.

She had, however, read about the one owned by Queen Victoria.

'It is like a dolls'-house,' she said to the Earl.

'I usually use it only on long journeys,' the Earl explained, 'but as my Grandmother was coming, I wanted to be sure she would be comfortable.'

'I think it is wonderful of her to come,' Lupita answered, 'but I am afraid she will find, because I have been away, that the household is rather upset.'

'Grandmama will not mind,' the Earl said, 'and you do realise that it means you will be correctly and properly chaperoned?'

It was something Lupita had not thought of, and for a moment she looked surprised.

Then she said slowly:

'I ... I suppose ... people would think it ... wrong for you to stay at Wood Hall ... without one.'

'It is not *I* who will be chaperoned, but *you*,' the Earl laughed, 'and of course we must do what is correct.'

He thought when it became known that he had stayed at Wood Hall it would certainly fan the gossip about their being engaged.

In telling Mrs Asquith at the Devonshire House Ball that they were engaged, he had just been striking out at Heloise.

He had not really considered the consequences of his action.

Now he knew it was something he would not have done had he been thinking clearly, because eventually it must hurt Lupita.

She was so young and unsophisticated.

He was now ashamed of himself for doing anything that might besmirch her reputation.

Then he told himself he must find her a husband who would look after her and protect her against her Cousin, as well, he added, as any other man who might in any way upset or endanger her.

The whistle blew and the train started off.

As Lupita sat beside his Grandmother, talking to her with shining eyes, he thought what a sweet temperament she had.

She would certainly, he felt, make some man very happy.

'She belongs to the country,' he decided,

'and it would be a mistake for her to become spoilt in London.'

It gave him a feeling of satisfaction to remember that when Anthony Benson arrived later in the afternoon, it would be to find that 'the bird had flown.'

'Serve him right!' the Earl thought somewhat childishly. 'He should not have proposed to the girl on such short acquaintance.'

He could not help wondering how many men in the future would want to marry Lupita.

He had not missed the looks she had received last night, not only from the younger men, but also the older ones.

As he sat down at the card-table, the three men with him all had said that without exception she was the prettiest girl they had seen in years.

One man went on:

'I was extremely fond of her Father. He was a Gentleman in every sense of the word, which is more than I can say for some of the younger generation!'

'I agree with you,' another man said, 'and his wife was the kindest, sweetest woman that ever graced a dining-table.'

The third man laughed.

'That sounds as if you were in love with her yourself!'

'She was older than I was, and I think every man at that time fell in love with her. But unlike

110

so many "Beauties," she only ever looked at her husband, whom she adored.'

Listening to them, the Earl thought that was exactly what he wanted for himself.

Judging by his experience with Heloise, however, he doubted if he would ever find it.

Because even to think of her made him angry, he had said:

'Come on! Let us get on with the game, otherwise we will have to go back to the Ball-Room before we have finished it.'

Now he decided that he would not have Lupita upset by her unpleasant Cousin.

He would give Rufus Lang a 'piece of his mind' when he got to Wood Hall.

They had luncheon on the train.

It had been provided in a great hurry by the Earl's Cook at Grosvenor Square, but it was delicious.

But Lupita found it hard to eat it because she was worrying about what she would find when they reached her home.

It was an irrepressible relief to know that the Earl was with her.

At the same time, she was afraid their treasures might already have been sold.

If Rufus had managed to break open the safe, the jewellery would have gone too.

Even if the Earl drove him away, she wondered how she would be able to keep everything intact for Jerry.

There might be other men, apart from

Rufus, who would try to cheat him out of his inheritance.

How could she be strong enough to prevent it?

She must have been looking worried, for the Dowager Countess said to her:

'Just trust Ingram, dearest child. He will put everything right.'

'I am ... sure it is ... upsetting for him to have to ... leave London when he has ... so many engagements,' Lupita answered.

The Earl was standing at a window, pointing out to Jerry a Castle as they passed by it.

The Dowager Countess lowered her voice so that her grandson could not hear, and said:

'To be frank with you, my dear, I am delighted to see him with another interest rather than that fast young woman with whom he has been associating. I always disliked her, and the fact that she is to be married to someone else is a great relief.'

'She ... she made ... me feel as if I had ... done something ... wrong,' Lupita said hesitatingly.

'I heard about that,' the Dowager Countess answered, 'and I promise you, my dear, you did nothing wrong. You were in fact a great success and your Father and Mother would have been proud of you.'

Lupita smiled.

'That is what I ... wanted to hear, Ma'am, and thank you ... thank ... you for coming to

Wood Hall! But I do hope it will . . . not tire . . . you.'

'I do not tire when I am enjoying myself,' the Dowager Countess replied, 'and that, believe it or not, is what I am doing at the moment.'

As the smile came back into Lupita's eyes, she thought it would be impossible to find a more charming girl.

Then she sighed and added to herself:

'But it is unlikely that my grandson will think so, seeing where his interest has lain in the past.'

They arrived at Wood Hall at four o'clock.

Owing to the Earl's excellent powers of organisation, there were carriages to meet them from the nearest Livery Stable.

Lupita was about to exclaim that she should have arranged for the carriages to come from Wood Hall.

Then she realised that the Earl intended to take her Cousin Rufus by surprise.

He would through this arrangement have no inkling that they were arriving.

Mr Matthews had, of course, travelled in the train with the Dowager Countess's lady's-maid and the Earl's Valet.

As Lupita watched them get out, she was aware there was also one of the Earl's Senior Footmen with them.

'We will certainly be arriving in style!' she told herself.

She could not help feeling with satisfaction

113

that it would be a shock to Cousin Rufus to see them.

'I am ... sure the Earl will be ... able to ... frighten him away,' she thought happily.

As she looked at him waiting to get into the carriage, she knew he was undoubtedly the most wonderful man she could possibly imagine.

CHAPTER SIX

Jerry scrambled into the carriage with his dog.

The Earl looked back to see that the other carriage was being filled up with the servants and the luggage.

He then looked at the inside of the slightly ancient carriage in which his Grandmother and Lupita were sitting, and said:

'I think to be comfortable, I will sit between two beautiful women.'

His Grandmother laughed.

'I am sure Lupita and I can make ourselves small enough so as not to crush you,' she said.

The Earl climbed in and sat down between them.

There was, in fact, plenty of room, as it was an old-fashioned carriage.

Jerry spread himself out comfortably with *Bracken* beside him, and remarked:

'He knows he is going home.'

Lupita tried to feel excited by the idea, but was too apprehensive.

She was afraid of what could happen when she arrived, knowing that Cousin Rufus would be extremely annoyed at their appearing so unexpectedly.

As they drove off, the Earl must have realised what she was feeling, for he put his hand over hers and said:

'Do not worry. Leave everything to me. It will not be as bad as you fear.'

She thought it was like him to be aware of what she was feeling.

As his fingers tightened for a moment on her hand, she felt a strange feeling move through her like a flash of lightning.

She could hardly believe it was happening.

At the same time, she knew it was because the Earl was so close to her and was touching her.

It was then she realised for the first time that she loved him.

It seemed to her as if thrills streaked through her body.

'I love him . . . I love him!' she thought. 'But I never knew it until now.'

She thought about it as they drove on, and knew now she had loved him when every night she had thanked God that he was protecting her.

She had loved him when they danced together, and had been very excited to have his arms around her waist.

'Of course I love him,' she told herself. 'How could I not, when he is so magnificent, and at the same time so understanding?'

The Earl took his hand from hers and they drove on.

She was telling herself that when all this was over he would go back to London and forget about her.

He would be with women like Heloise Brook, who was so beautiful and sophisticated, to amuse him.

'What have I to look forward to in the future?' Lupita thought miserably.

She told herself severely that she had to be sensible.

If he ever loved somebody, it would be, as she had said herself, somebody important, perhaps even a Princess.

Nevertheless, whatever happened, she told herself, she would still have these moments with him.

At least they would be something to remember.

Now they were moving through familiar countryside, and she wanted to point out to the Earl how beautiful it was.

There were fields yellow with buttercups and hedgerows thick with honeysuckle.

Then she told herself that this was her world.

His was very different.

'You are very silent, Lupita!' the Earl remarked unexpectedly. 'I thought by now you would be telling me when we were on your Estate and showing me the first glimpse of your home.'

'I want to do that,' Lupita replied, 'and we are nearly there.'

'When we get home,' Jerry said, 'you must come and see *Sambo*. He is a very big horse and I can ride him. In a year or so I am going to

117

have an even bigger horse!'

'I am sure you will,' the Earl said, 'and if you ride as well as your Father, everybody will be very proud of you.'

Jerry put his arm round *Bracken*.

'When I am grown up,' he said, 'I am going to have hundreds of horses and hundreds of dogs, all my own!'

'Well, I hope your horses win every race in which you enter them,' the Earl said.

'I hope so too,' Jerry replied.

The Earl turned to his Grandmother.

'You are not feeling too tired, Grandmama?'

'I am looking forward more than I can say to seeing Wood Hall,' she replied. 'I often wondered if it was as beautiful as Lupita's Mother. I felt that somehow it must be a frame for her beauty.'

'I do hope you will not be disappointed,' Lupita said.

'I am sure I shall not be,' the Dowager Countess said firmly.

A few minutes later Lupita was able to point out to the Earl the boundary of the Wood Hall Estate.

Because the fields were well cultivated, the hedges clipped, and the view very lovely, she felt proud of all Jerry owned.

At last they came to the small village built near the Park, and Lupita thought the Earl would appreciate the gardens filled with flowers.

They turned in at the lodge gates, and as they moved down the drive the house came into view.

It did indeed look very beautiful with the afternoon sun shining on the windows.

It was a Tudor mansion, and the bricks over the centuries had become a warm pink.

There was a gabled roof and the back of the house was protected by trees.

It was the Dowager Countess who spoke first.

'It is lovely!' she said. 'Just as I thought it would be.'

'Thank you,' Lupita said.

'Now that Papa is dead, it is my house,' Jerry said solemnly.

'You must take good care of it,' the Dowager Countess observed, 'and see that it always looks as beautiful as it does today.'

The carriage stopped at the front entrance, and as it did so Lupita was hoping they would not be disillusioned by what they saw inside.

The Earl got out and helped first his Grandmother, then Lupita to alight.

As he was doing so, the front-door opened and Briggs, the old Butler, stood looking at them in astonishment.

Then, as he saw Lupita, he hurried down the steps.

'Your Ladyship!' he exclaimed. 'I was not expecting you!'

'We have come home, Briggs,' Lupita said,

'and brought some guests with us.'

Before Briggs could say anything, she asked in a low voice:

'Where is Mr Rufus?'

'He's not here at the moment, M'Lady,' Briggs replied. Then, dropping his voice, he added: 'He's gone to find a Locksmith in the Town who'll open the safe.'

The Earl heard what he said and without speaking continued to help his Grandmother up the steps and into the hall.

When the Dowager Countess saw the ancient panelling on the walls and its medieval fireplace and the oak staircase with its carved banisters, she gave a cry of delight.

'It is just as I imagined it would be,' she said.

'I'll lay tea in the Drawing-Room, M'Lady,' Briggs said to Lupita. 'It'll take me a minute or so.'

'Thank you, Briggs,' Lupita said, 'and ask your wife to take Her Ladyship's lady's-maid to the best bedroom.'

Briggs nodded as if that was what he had already decided was correct.

They went across the hall and the Dowager Countess was already exclaiming at the beauty of the Drawing-Room with its large diamond-paned windows and tapestry chairs.

The Earl, however, said in a low voice to Lupita:

'Shall I go and see what has been put on the Billiard-table?'

'Yes, please do,' she answered.

As he turned to leave the room, she gave a little exclamation of horror.

'Papa's collection of ... snuff-boxes has gone from here,' she said, 'and also the Sèvres china.'

The Earl did not reply.

He merely said to Briggs, who was just about to go upstairs:

'Show me the way to the Billiard-Room.'

He thought the man looked at him indecisively.

'Of course, Her Ladyship has not told you the names of her guests!' he said. 'We are the Dowager Countess and the Earl of Ardwick. As I knew Her Ladyship's Father, I am now acting as her Guardian.'

'That's good news, M'Lord, very good news!' Briggs said. 'There be things goin' on here as would make His Lordship turn in his grave!'

'So I understand,' the Earl said, 'so take me to the Billiard-Room.'

Briggs took him down a long corridor and opened the door at the far end of it.

One glance told the Earl that Mr Matthews had not exaggerated about Rufus Lang's intentions.

The huge table was covered with what Lupita had referred to as the special treasures of the house.

There was the Sèvres china and the snuff-

121

boxes which must have come from the Drawing-Room.

There were gold carved mirrors and various other ancient and valuable *objets d'art*.

The Earl looked at it for a few minutes before he said:

'Have you other help in the house?'

'Yes, M'Lord,' Briggs replied. 'There's two young men as acts as footmen, but as Her Ladyship wasn't here, I let them go to the village where they comes from, to see their families.'

'As soon as they come back, have everything on this table put back in its rightful place,' the Earl ordered. 'In the meantime, now that I have seen what has been collected here, I want you to lock the door and give me the key.'

Briggs did as he was told, and as the Earl took the key and put it in his pocket, he asked:

'Has anything been sold?'

'No, M'Lord,' Briggs replied. 'Mr Rufus were waiting to get the safe opened before he sent for the men from London to see the silver and the jewellery as belonged to Her Ladyship's Mother.'

'I heard about that from Mr Matthews,' the Earl said. 'I must compliment you on your quick-wittedness in keeping the key from him. It was extremely intelligent of you, and Her Ladyship is very grateful.'

'Mr Rufus tried shooting off the lock, M'Lord, but it wouldn' budge, an' that's why he's gone into the Town for the Locksmith.'

'You can tell him that will not be necessary,' the Earl said, 'and I wish to see Mr Rufus as soon as he comes back.'

'Very good, M'Lord.'

Briggs was obviously delighted at having someone in authority, and he smiled as he hurried to the kitchen to order tea.

He also unlocked the safe and took out the beautiful Georgian silver tea-service which Lupita's Mother had always used.

When the Earl went back to the Drawing-Room, Lupita looked at him enquiringly.

'Nothing has been sold, so do not worry,' he said quietly, 'and now that we are here, everything will be restored to its rightful place.'

Lupita looked at him, but could not find words in which to tell him how grateful she was.

He thought no woman had ever looked at him with such an expression of veneration.

It made him feel almost as if he were a God from Olympus.

Jerry came running into the Drawing-Room with *Bracken* at his heels.

'We are home! We are home,' he cried as if he had suddenly become aware of the fact, 'and I want to show you *Sambo*.'

'I think we just have time to do so before Briggs brings in the tea,' Lupita said as she smiled.

She looked enquiringly at the Earl as she

spoke, feeling that because he had taken charge, she must ask his permission before they did anything.

'I will come with you,' he said, 'and I will be very interested to see your Father's horses.'

'I am longing to show you the stables,' Lupita said. 'My Father designed them himself, and while the house is very old, the stables are quite new.'

'Then I must certainly see them,' the Earl agreed.

It was only a short distance to walk round to the back of the house and through an archway to the cobbled yard of the stables.

Jerry ran ahead to find *Sambo*.

As they went, Lupita explained to the Earl how her Father had used the old buildings, enlarged them, and fitted them out inside in a very modern and up-to-date manner.

The Earl, who had made a great many renovations in his own stables, was very impressed.

The stalls were larger than was usual, and a new type of manger had been fitted into each one.

The horses' names were printed outside their doors, with a history of their breeding.

On the wall of the passage opposite the stalls were hung the animals' bridles and saddles.

They had been hung there so that it was easy to lift them down and clean them.

'Papa thought that each horse should get

used to one particular saddle,' Lupita explained, 'and think of it as his own, just as we prefer our own clothes.'

'That is an excellent idea, and one I will copy,' the Earl replied.

She went on to show him many other innovations.

There was the way the water was supplied which made the mucking out of the stables easier, and she was delighted to see that the Earl was suitably impressed.

When they reached *Sambo*'s stall, she allowed Jerry to show him to the Earl.

Sambo was, as the Earl recognised, a very fine and well-trained animal and exactly right for a small boy.

He thought that if he had a son, he would like him to be as enthusiastic and thrilled by having his own horse as Jerry was.

There was not enough time to see all the horses, since Lupita thought they should go back and have tea with the Dowager Countess.

She was also afraid that her Cousin Rufus might turn up and make trouble before the Earl was actually there.

As they were leaving the stables, Lupita thought that Jerry would be reluctant to leave *Sambo*.

But he patted him and said:

'I will come back and say goodnight to you.'

As they walked back to the house, Lupita was aware that the Earl was looking at the lake.

She did not say anything, but she was sure he was remembering what she had told him about Rufus damaging the boat.

As they entered the Drawing-Room, it was to find that Briggs had already laid the table.

The silver tea-pot, kettle, and sugar-bowl were standing on a beautiful tray.

A young footman was putting cakes and sandwiches on the table beside them.

'I must say I am looking forward to a cup of tea,' the Dowager Countess said. 'Then I am going to lie down before dinner.'

She put up her hand to prevent her grandson from saying anything, and went on:

'Do not suggest that I do not come down again, because I have every intention of doing so to see what I am sure is a very beautiful Dining-Room, and also to enjoy the company of you both.'

'We look forward to entertaining you, Grandmama,' the Earl said, 'and I assure you, we want you to be with us.'

'That is a compliment which I appreciate,' the Dowager Countess said.

She enjoyed her tea, and Jerry tasted everything that was on the table.

Lupita, however, could not help listening for the sound of footsteps in the hall.

She was wondering how soon Cousin Rufus would return.

But there was no sign of him, and as soon as tea was finished, the Dowager Countess went upstairs.

Lupita went with her to escort her to her room.

Mrs Briggs had put the Dowager Countess in Lupita's Mother's room.

It was undoubtedly the prettiest bedroom in the house, and Lupita knew that the Dowager Countess's expression of delight was sincere.

Her lady's-maid was waiting, having unpacked everything she needed.

Lupita told the lady's-maid to ask for anything she needed, then went to her own room.

She remembered how frightened she had been the last time she had left it.

What had occurred since then in London now seemed all part of a dream.

Could she really have been a success so that people admired her and she had even had a proposal of marriage?

It was difficult now to believe it was all true.

Having tidied herself, she wanted to go downstairs again to be with the Earl.

It was as she reached the top of the stairs that she heard a carriage draw up outside.

A moment later Rufus Lang walked in through the front-door.

Lupita did not make a sound or move, but he looked up and saw her.

For a moment he just stared. Then he said angrily:

'So you are back! What the devil do you

mean by running off like that?'

Lupita did not answer, but the sound of his voice alerted the Earl, for he came out of the Drawing-Room.

'Good-evening, Lang,' he said. 'I think we have met before. As you see, I have brought Lady Lupita and her brother home, and my Grandmother, the Dowager Countess, is also with us.'

Rufus Lang made no pretence of not recognising the Earl.

'I cannot imagine, Ardwick, how you have become involved in this,' he remarked.

'If you will come into the Drawing-Room, I will tell you how it concerns me,' the Earl replied.

Lupita thought it would be a mistake for her to join them.

But Rufus Lang looked up at her and said:

'As you are responsible for this intrusion, you had better come and explain what has been happening.'

Lupita drew in her breath.

She came down the stairs, aware that Rufus Lang was waiting for her and did not intend to be alone in the Drawing-Room with the Earl.

The Earl had already walked back into the room, and when Lupita and her Cousin came in, he was standing with his back to the mantelpiece.

As Briggs shut the door behind them, Rufus Lang said:

'I do not wish to seem rude, but I cannot quite understand why you, in your busy life, should be concerned with my young Cousins.'

'I have appointed myself as Guardian to these two young people,' the Earl explained in a lofty tone, 'for the simple reason that I think they are both in need of protection.'

'I do not know what you mean by that!' Rufus Lang said.

There was an ugly note in his voice, and Lupita was aware that he was looking somewhat threateningly at the Earl.

'Then let me start by telling you,' the Earl said, 'that I have given orders for everything that you have had put on the Billiard-table to be returned to its proper place!'

Rufus Lang lost his temper.

'Curse you for interfering!' he said angrily. 'You are not related to my family, and if anyone should have the position as Guardian, it should be me!'

'A Guardian who is prepared to rob the young innocents he is supposed to be guarding?' the Earl asked sharply.

There was a moment's silence.

Then, as Rufus Lang could not think of a suitable reply, the Earl said:

'I think, Lang, that the sooner you leave here, the better. And let me make it perfectly clear that if you come here again, or touch anything that is the property of the present Earl of Langwood, I will take you to the

Courts.'

Rufus Lang was defeated, and he knew it.

With a quick change of mood he said:

'All right, I made a mistake and I admit it. But I am desperately in need of cash and was thinking of the family name rather than of the needs of a small boy of six.'

The Earl did not reply, and after a somewhat uncomfortable silence, Rufus Lang went on:

'I will leave tomorrow, as soon as it is possible, but I do not particularly want to drive back to London tonight. The train, if there is one, will not get in until very late.'

He paused, looked at the Earl, then at Lupita.

'After all, I am your Cousin,' he said, 'and if you are throwing me to the dogs, or rather to the Duns, you might at least allow me to have a good dinner. It may be the last I shall enjoy for a very long time.'

Lupita did not know what to reply, but the Earl said:

'Very well. You can stay the night on condition that you leave immediately after breakfast. If you do that, I will give you enough money to get to London and at least afford a decent lodging, if you do not have one at the moment.'

'I am grateful, deeply grateful,' Rufus Lang said. 'I suppose we all make mistakes in our lives, and I admit I have made a number of very bad ones in mine.'

He sounded so contrite that Lupita thought it would be impossible for them to do anything but agree to what he asked.

She thought it very generous of the Earl to offer him financial help.

She was quite certain it would be enough to keep him for a week or two, at any rate.

Because she felt it was embarrassing to stay any longer, she walked towards the door.

Rufus opened it for her, saying as he did so in a low voice:

'Forgive me, Lupita. I know I have made a fool of myself, but I was desperate, absolutely desperate!'

'I am sorry,' Lupita said.

She did not want to say any more, and went upstairs.

She thought as she did so that if Rufus was staying for dinner, it would spoil the evening.

At the same time, she did not see how they could do anything but accept him.

The Earl was thinking the same thing.

As a matter of fact, he could not help feeling sorry for the young man, who had foolishly thrown away his money in gambling.

He decided he would give him a few hundred pounds which he hoped would keep him away from Wood Hall and Lupita.

Contrary to what Lupita had feared, dinner turned out to be quite an enjoyable meal.

The Dowager Countess, who did not know how badly Rufus had behaved, was charming to him.

He paid her compliments and put himself out to be agreeable in every possible way.

Even the Earl had to admit that he put on a very good show.

He told stories that made them laugh.

He talked to the Earl about his race-horses, a subject in which he obviously was well-informed, and he treated Jerry as if he was a grown-up.

Because dinner was early, Jerry had been allowed, as a special treat, to stay and dine with them.

When dinner was over, while the two gentlemen were left to their port, Lupita took Jerry upstairs to his room.

Bracken was already there, waiting for him.

'Tomorrow,' she said, 'we are going riding and the Earl will be able to see you on *Sambo*.'

'I know,' Jerry said, 'and he told me before dinner that he was a very fine horse. I said I would race him on one of Papa's horses.'

'I am afraid the Earl will win,' Lupita warned him with a smile.

'Not if he gives me a very big start,' Jerry answered.

'I am sure that is what he will do,' Lupita replied.

'It's fun being home,' Jerry said as he got into bed, 'and I hope the Earl will stay a long time. He knows lots and lots about horses!'

'Yes, he does,' Lupita answered.

She kissed her brother goodnight, then went downstairs again.

By this time the Earl and Rufus Lang were in the Drawing-Room with the Dowager Countess.

'Is your brother pleased to be home?' the Earl asked Lupita as she joined them.

'He is determined to race you tomorrow on *Sambo*,' Lupita replied, 'but he says you will have to give him a very big start!'

The Earl laughed.

'Of course I will do that, but it seems rather a big horse for such a small boy.'

'That is what I said,' Lupita agreed, 'but *Sambo* is such a well-trained horse that I am sure Jerry will come to no harm on him.'

'If he is becoming as good a rider as his Father,' the Earl answered, 'I do not think you need worry.'

Lupita smiled at him.

She thought as she did so that even to look at him made a thrill run through her body.

'He ... must never ... never know,' she told herself.

The Earl suggested that his Grandmother should have an early night.

He took her upstairs at half-past-ten and Lupita went with them.

She had no wish to be alone with Cousin Rufus.

As she followed the Earl and the Dowager Countess, she said:

'I am going to bed too, so goodnight, Cousin Rufus!'

'Goodnight, Lupita,' he said, 'and goodbye.'

She did not answer.

She felt a little guilty for being so glad that he was going.

She hoped she would never see him again.

Once her Cousin had left, she thought, he would be too frightened of the Earl ever to come back.

'We are safe! We are safe!' she told herself as she got into bed. 'And it is all thanks to the Earl.'

She felt a sharp tremor of fear that when the Earl went back to London, he would show no further interest in them.

Then she was sure if anything untowards happened in the future, she would always be able to call on him.

'I shall ... want to do ... that,' she added. 'I love him! I love him! It will be ... hard to ... go on without seeing him ... and without ... hearing his ... voice.'

The Earl talked to Rufus Lang mostly about horses, then he too said he was going to bed.

'I have had a number of late nights this week,' the Earl explained, 'and I shall be glad to get some sleep.'

He thought as he spoke that he was being somewhat pointedly unkind.

It was quite obvious that Rufus Lang would stay awake, worrying over his debts.

134

'He has to learn to stand on his own feet,' the Earl thought when he reached his own bedroom, 'but I will give him a certain amount of help for the children's sake.'

Dawkins was waiting for him, and the Earl said:

'I have a letter to write to my Solicitors, so do not wait up. I will put myself to bed.'

'Y'Lordship's sure you can do that?' Dawkins asked.

The Earl knew that Dawkins was only being facetious, and he merely replied:

'Call me at eight o'clock.'

The Earl sat down at a desk that was in a corner of the bedroom and wrote a letter to his Solicitors.

He told them that he was prepared to give Rufus Lang a monthly allowance.

This was on condition that he kept away from Wood Hall.

He was not to interfere in the lives of his Cousins—Lady Lupita Lang and her young brother, the Earl of Langwood.

If he did so, the allowance was to cease immediately.

He also told them to enquire into Mr Lang's debts.

If he was in any danger of being taken before the Magistrates, which would incur unwelcome publicity, he was to be informed.

It took him some time to compose the letter.

He debated with himself after it was finished

135

whether he would show it to Rufus Lang tonight or wait until the morning.

Then he told himself he would do it that night.

If Rufus Lang had any questions to ask, he could answer them.

He opened his bedroom door to find that the corridor was in darkness.

The only light came from the hall.

It was easy, however, to see his way to Rufus Lang's bedroom on the other side of the corridor.

The Earl walked towards it and knocked gently, but there was no reply.

He turned the handle and looked inside.

Rufus Lang was not there. He had not undressed, neither had the bed been slept in.

The Earl thought it was strange.

Rufus Lang had come upstairs at the same time as he had.

He thought he might have gone back to the Drawing-Room, although it seemed unlikely.

Because he was curious, the Earl went down the stairs.

As he reached the hall, he noticed that the front-door was unbolted.

He knew that the door had been bolted when he went upstairs to bed.

Rufus Lang had gone out.

It seemed an odd thing to do, especially as he had said he was tired.

The Earl could not believe that he had gone

136

down to look at the boat which Lupita told him he had deliberately damaged.

But the Earl could think of no other explanation.

Why should Lang want to go into the garden at this time of night?

Could he, after all he had said, really be planning another murder?

On an impulse, the Earl walked out through the front-door and down the steps.

The stars were out and a moon climbing up the sky made it easy for him to see.

There were many shadows, but it did not seem as if there were any human beings about.

The Earl had a sudden feeling which he found difficult to explain to himself that he should go to the stables.

He walked round the house and through the archway.

He saw a light in the first stable in which there were eight horses.

The Earl stopped and took off his evening-shoes.

Walking silently in his stockinged feet and carrying his shoes, he went towards the stables.

The door was open and he slipped through it.

As he did so, he was aware that the light he had seen shining through the window came from a lantern in the passage.

Beside it was a man with his back to him.

The Earl knew it was Rufus Lang.

He was doing something outside the stall where *Sambo* was stabled.

Silently the Earl moved into a corner of the stable where there was a stack of straw.

Still without making any sound, he hid himself behind it.

CHAPTER SEVEN

The Earl waited five minutes until Rufus Lang finished what he was doing.

Picking up the lantern, he walked down the passage.

Peeping at him through the straw, Earl saw him put back the lantern where it belonged above the entrance.

He then went out into the yard.

The Earl saw him pass the windows before there was silence.

The Earl was sensible enough not to move for some time.

Then he came from his hiding-place and, taking down the lantern, walked to *Sambo*'s stall.

He looked round, trying to imagine what Rufus Lang had been doing.

He took *Sambo*'s saddle down from the bar on which it hung and examined it.

He did not know what he was looking for.

He just felt it was the only thing which could have occupied Rufus Lang for so long.

Then, on the underside of the saddle, in the centre towards the back, he saw a small slit.

At first he just stared at it, then he suddenly guessed what Rufus Lang had been doing.

When he had been in America, the Earl had been shown by the cowboys what they sometimes did to a horse that had no spirit in him.

It was cruel, admittedly, but they caught an insect rather like a wasp and inserted it into the saddle.

When the horse was ridden, after a short time the insect would manage to get out of the hole and sting the horse's back.

In most cases the horse would buck and rear and behave in a wild manner because of the pain.

The cowboys thought it amusing to compete in trying to remain in the saddle in almost impossible circumstances.

The Earl's lips tightened with fury.

He realised that this was another way by which Lang hoped to kill Jerry.

His first impulse was to pull what he supposed must be a wasp out of the saddle and stamp on it.

Then he had another idea.

Carrying *Sambo*'s saddle, he took it to where one belonging to a young, rather high-spirited horse was hanging.

He made a note of the name on the stall, which was *Knight Star*.

He made a slit in this horse's saddle, prised out the wasp from *Sambo*'s saddle without killing it, then inserted it into *Knight Star*'s saddle.

He then returned both saddles to their correct places and replaced the lantern.

140

As he made his way back to the house, he guessed that Rufus Lang would enter through the front-door and bolt it again.

He therefore went to a side door which was not far from the Pantry and knocked.

When he had knocked twice, the door was opened by a sleepy footman.

He had been given orders by Briggs to guard the safe.

As the Earl walked inside, he said:

'I went for a walk and forgot that the front-door would be locked by now. I am sorry if I woke you up.'

'Tha's all right, M'Lord,' the footman answered.

The Earl gave him a guinea and he gasped with delight.

'As I do not want Her Ladyship to be upset by learning I was locked out,' he said, 'keep what happened to yourself.'

'Oi'll do tha', M'Lord,' the footman said as he grinned.

The Earl went up a side staircase.

As he expected, everything was quiet.

No-one saw him as he moved silently back into his bedroom.

*　　　*　　　*

The next morning Jerry was up before anybody else, talking excitedly about his ride on *Sambo*.

'Did you tell the Earl I want to race him?' he

141

asked Lupita.

'I did,' she answered, 'but you will have to be very clever to beat him.'

'I will whisper in *Sambo*'s ear that it is very important that he does,' Jerry said.

He ran down into the Breakfast-Room before anyone else.

When Lupita came down she found that not only the Earl but also Cousin Rufus was there.

She looked at him in surprise, thinking he should have left by then.

The Earl explained:

'I am told that the best train to London does not go until midday, so I thought it only fair to ask your Cousin to join our ride this morning.'

Lupita thought it was the last thing she wanted.

But she could only say that she hoped he would enjoy it.

'As it will be the last memory I have of Wood Hall, it is one I shall always cherish,' Rufus Lang replied.

She thought he was being somewhat melodramatic and concentrated on choosing what she would eat.

When breakfast was over, they all four went outside to where the horses were waiting for them.

'I hope you do not mind,' the Earl said to Lupita, 'but I sent a message by my Valet this morning to say I would like to ride that very handsome stallion which I am told your Father bought eighteen months ago at Tattersall's.'

He smiled at her before he went on:

'I think his name is *Mercury*. I also suggested *Knight Star* for your Cousin. Jerry of course will ride *Sambo*, and you told me that you always ride *Minerva*.'

'Certainly *Mercury* and *Knight Star* are two of our finest horses,' Lupita said as she smiled.

'That is what I thought myself,' the Earl replied.

He looked at *Sambo* as he did so, and Jerry said:

'I have told *Sambo* we have to beat you.'

'I only hope he obeys you,' Lupita laughed, 'but it is more important for the Earl to see how well you can ride.'

Jerry bent forward to pat *Sambo's* neck.

The Earl helped Lupita into *Minerva's* saddle.

As he walked towards *Mercury*, he suddenly realised that *Knight Star* was moving about restlessly.

Quite suddenly the horse reared, then bucked, and Rufus had great difficulty in staying in the saddle.

As the others watched him, *Knight Star* started forward, only to rear again and buck violently.

'What is wrong with *Knight Star*?' Jerry asked. 'Why is he behaving like that?'

There was no chance for the Earl to reply.

Knight Star was bucking in such a manner

that not even the most experienced horseman would have been able to keep him under control.

He galloped off to the edge of the courtyard, where there were flagstones.

He reared again and flung off his rider.

As Rufus Lang fell to the ground, *Knight Star* slipped and fell heavily on top of him.

Then he rolled over and over backwards and forwards, crushing the man beneath him.

Watching, the Earl made no effort to move or to stop the horse.

Then suddenly there was a scream from behind him and he turned round.

To his horror, he realised that *Minerva* was behaving in the same way as *Knight Star*.

She was rearing and bucking.

The Earl instantly realised what was wrong.

It had never occurred to him for a moment that Lang would try to kill not only Jerry, but also his sister.

With the swiftness of an athlete, he dashed forward as *Minerva* bucked and bucked again.

He caught hold of Lupita and dragged her from the saddle.

Even as he did so, *Minerva* shot away, rushing down towards the lake.

Just before the mare reached it, she started to roll over and over on the grass, just as *Knight Star* had done.

The Earl held Lupita very close to him.

She was almost fainting with fright.

At the same time, she was aware that his arms were round her and she was safe.

Carrying her, the Earl hurried back towards the house.

As he reached the steps, Lupita stirred and he said:

'It is all right, my darling, you are quite safe and so is Jerry.'

She wanted to ask him what had happened, but the words would not come to her lips.

She was badly shocked and frightened.

The Earl could feel her whole body trembling against him.

He took her into the hall just as Briggs and the footmen came rushing out to see what was happening.

The Earl glanced back to see that a groom was holding *Sambo* while Jerry stared in amazement at the two other horses.

Carrying Lupita, the Earl walked across the hall and into the Drawing-Room.

He sat on the sofa, holding her in his arms as if she were a child.

Her head was against his shoulder.

After a few moments she managed to look up at him and ask in a voice he could hardly hear:

'Wh-what ... h-happened?'

'How could I have been such a fool,' the Earl exclaimed, 'as not to realise your Cousin would try to kill you too!'

'B-but ... you ... s-saved me!' she whispered.

145

He looked down into her eyes.

Then he was kissing her.

Kissing her as if he were afraid he might have lost her and could not express his relief in any other way.

To Lupita it was as if Heaven had opened and he had taken her inside.

She could feel the thrill she had felt before seeping through her body.

She thought she would awake to find this was all a dream.

Only as the Earl raised his head did she know that it was real.

'Y-you ... kissed me!' she said in a rapt little whisper.

'I love you, my darling,' the Earl said, 'but through my own stupidity I nearly lost you!'

He kissed her again, a long, passionate kiss.

It made her feel that he took her heart and her soul from her body and made it his.

As if she could not help it, she asked once again:

'Wh-what ... happened? Why did ... *Knight Star* and *Minerva* go ... mad?'

'Your Cousin had intended it to happen not to *Knight Star* but to *Sambo*,' the Earl said.

'Oh ... no ... no! How could ... he do ... anything ... so ... so wicked ... so cruel?'

'Very fortunately I discovered last night what he was doing,' the Earl went on, 'but I did not think to look at your saddle as well as *Sambo's*.'

146

'What ... had he ... d-done to the ... saddle? I do not ... understand.'

'I will explain later,' the Earl said. 'All that matters for the moment is that you are safe. And, unless I am very much mistaken, your Cousin is dead.'

'D-dead!' Lupita exclaimed.

'If not, he will be crippled for life, and I think in the circumstances any man would rather die.'

'H-he ... meant ... that to h-happen to ... Jerry!'

Lupita could hardly say the words, and the Earl's arms tightened.

'It is something you must try to forget,' he said, 'but now Jerry is safe, and so, my precious one, are you!'

Lupita looked up at him.

'You ... saved Jerry ... too! How can ... you be so ... so wonderful?'

'Since that is how I want you to think of me,' the Earl said, 'how soon will you marry me?'

Lupita was still.

Then she questioned:

'Did ... you ... really ... ask me ... to m-marry ... you?'

'I intend to marry you immediately,' the Earl asserted, 'and, as your Guardian, I can recommend the Earl of Ardwick as a very suitable husband!'

There was laughter in his voice.

But the expression in his eyes told Lupita he

147

really loved her.

'I … I knew … yesterday,' she murmured, 'that … I have … loved you for a … long time … but I never … never thought that … you would … love me.'

'I have been fighting against my feelings for you,' the Earl said, 'but when I thought that Devil was going to destroy you, I knew that I could not go on living without you.'

'How can … you say … anything so … marvellous?' Lupita asked.

'I have a great deal more to say,' the Earl answered, 'but I think, my darling, if you feel strong enough, we should go and look after Jerry, and I must arrange either for your Cousin to be taken to a Hospital, or for a coffin to be made for him.'

Lupita gave a little shudder.

If it had not been for his foresight, the Earl would have been saying that about herself and Jerry.

As if he did not wish her to think of such things, the Earl kissed her again.

Then he rose from the sofa and drew her to her feet.

'On second thought,' he said, 'I want you to stay here. There is no need for you to see what has happened outside. I will send Jerry in to you.'

Lupita put out her hands towards him.

'You will … not be … long?' she questioned.

'I will come back to you as quickly as I can,'

the Earl promised. 'I have a great deal to tell you about how much I love you and how beautiful you are.'

As he finished speaking, he kissed her forehead.

Then with what seemed to be an effort, he walked towards the door.

Because she hardly knew what she was doing, Lupita sat down again on the sofa.

Everything that had happened seemed so incredible that it was hard to think clearly.

But all that really mattered was that the Earl loved her as she loved him.

They were to be married.

She thought that her Father and Mother were pleased that she had found such a perfect husband.

She felt as if they were near her at this moment, smiling at her happiness.

It must have been her Father, she thought, who had sent the Earl into her life and enabled him to save Jerry and herself.

'Thank you ... thank you ... Papa,' she whispered, 'and ... please tell ... God how ... grateful I ... am.'

* * *

When the Dowager Countess was told the whole story, she found it hard to believe.

Then the Earl said that he and Lupita were to be married, and she cried from sheer happiness.

'Lupita is exactly the sort of wife I have always wanted for you, Ingram,' she said. 'I was so afraid you would marry one of those hard women who wanted to marry you only for your title.'

'I do not think that is a very flattering remark, Grandmama!' the Earl teased. 'But I know what you mean.'

'I told him he should ... marry a ... Princess,' Lupita said, 'but perhaps because I love him so much he will not realise how unimportant I am.'

The Earl put out his hand to take hers.

'To me you are the most important person in the world,' he said, 'and as for marrying a Princess, I am marrying the Queen of my Heart, and what man could ask for more?'

'That was a very pretty speech!' his Grandmother approved.

'There is ... only one thing that ... worries me,' Lupita said hesitatingly.

'What is that?' the Earl asked.

'What is ... going to happen ... to ... Jerry?'

'I have been thinking about that myself,' the Earl answered.

'Well, I have a solution,' the Dowager Countess said. 'As you know, I have always disliked the Dower House which was built only fifty years ago and is, in my opinion, very ugly.'

She paused a moment and then continued:

'If Lupita will allow me, I would love to

come to live here at Wood Hall. It is exactly the sort of home I have always envisaged for myself.'

She touched Lupita's cheek and went on softly:

'And I cannot help thinking that Lupita's Mother would be glad that I was looking after Jerry as well as the house.'

Lupita's eyes were shining.

'Do you ... really mean that ... Ma'am?' she asked. 'It would be ... perfect for me to know that ... you were ... here.'

'We will come and stay with you very often,' the Earl added, 'and Jerry can spend his time between here and with us at Ardwick Park.'

He smiled as he added:

'I think he will enjoy the horses in both places, and so will my sons, when you give them to me.'

He put his arm round Lupita as he spoke.

She blushed as she pressed her cheek against his shoulder.

'We will have ... dozens and ... dozens of ... children,' she murmured.

The Earl laughed.

'I will be content with a dozen, but if they all want horses to ride, we shall have to enlarge the stables!'

'You are going too fast,' the Dowager Countess said. 'At the same time, I am so glad that you approve of my idea, and I will look forward to having Jerry with me, and, of course, as many great-grandchildren as you can give me!'

The Earl bent and kissed her.

'I might have known, Grandmama, that you would solve the problem, just as you used to when I was a little boy.'

'The only real problem, as far as I was concerned,' his Grandmother replied, 'was that you would marry the wrong person! As it is, I could not be more delighted with my new granddaughter!'

Lupita kissed her and felt that in many ways she resembled her own Mother.

Certainly the house seemed exactly right for her, just as it had been exactly right for the beautiful Countess of Langwood.

That evening, after the Dowager Countess and Jerry had gone to bed, the Earl and Lupita were alone in the Drawing-Room.

He led her to the window that was open, and they stood looking up at the stars.

The Earl drew Lupita closer to him.

'It is a beautiful night, my darling, and you are the star who will guide me and help me all through the years that lay ahead of us.'

'I ... think ... I will be ... following you ... not leading ... you,' Lupita corrected the Earl.

'I want you to do that. At the same time, I know that ever since I met you I have felt inspired in a different way than I have ever been before. There are a great many things we can do together not only to help ourselves but

152

also to help our country.'

He spoke very solemnly, and Lupita gave a little cry of joy.

'That is what I ... wanted you ... to say,' she answered, 'and because you are so ... wonderful I must not be ... greedy and keep ... you *all* to ... myself.'

'I may need my brain for other people,' the Earl said, 'but you know, my darling, my heart is completely and absolutely yours, and nothing will ever alter that!'

Tears came into Lupita's eyes as she asked:

'H-how can I ... be so lucky?'

'I think that what lies beyond the stars,' the Earl said quietly, 'has brought us together.'

He looked lovingly at her before he continued: 'We were made for each other, you and I, and between us we must help to rid the world of evil, and bring beauty and love to all those who need it.'

There was nothing Lupita could say, so she raised her lips to his.

Then he was kissing her, at first gently, then passionately.

She knew they had found the real Love which all men seek, and a few are fortunate enough to find.

It is the Love unchanging and everlasting that comes from beyond the stars.

ABOUT THE AUTHOR

Barbara Cartland, the world's most famous romantic novelist, who is also an historian, playwright, lecturer, political speaker and television personality, has now written 617 books and sold over six hundred and twenty million copies all over the world.

She has also had many historical works published and has written four autobiographies as well as the biographies of her mother and that of her brother, Ronald Cartland, who was the first Member of Parliament to be killed in the last war. This book has a preface by Sir Winston Churchill and has been republished with an introduction by Sir Arthur Bryant.

Love at the Helm, a novel written with the help and inspiration of the late Earl Mountbatten of Burma, Great Uncle of His Royal Highness, The Prince of Wales, is being sold for the Mountbatten Memorial Trust.

She has broken the world record for the last twenty-one years by writing an average of twenty-three books a year. In the *Guinness Book of World Records* she is listed as the world's top-selling author.

Miss Cartland in 1987 sang an Album of Love Songs with the Royal Philharmonic Orchestra.

In private life Barbara Cartland, who is a Dame of the Order of St John of Jerusalem and Chairman of the St John Council in Hertfordshire, has fought for better conditions and salaries for Midwives and Nurses.

She championed the cause for the Elderly in 1956, invoking a Government Enquiry into the 'Housing Condition of Old People.'

In 1962 she had the Law of England changed so that Local Authorities had to provide camps for their own Gypsies. This has meant that since then thousands and thousands of Gypsy children have been able to go to School, which they had never been able to do in the past, as their caravans were moved every twenty-four hours by the Police.

There are now fifteen camps in Hertfordshire and Barbara Cartland has her own Romany Gypsy Camp called 'Barbaraville' by the Gypsies.

Her designs 'Decorating with Love' are being sold all over the U.S.A. and the National Home Fashions League made her, in 1981, 'Woman of Achievement.'

She is unique in that she was one and two in the Dalton list of Best Sellers, and one week had four books in the top twenty.

Barbara Cartland's book *Getting Older, Growing Younger* has been published in Great Britain and the U.S.A. and her fifth cookery book, *The Romance of Food*, is now being used by the House of Commons.

In 1984 she received at Kennedy Airport America's Bishop Wright Air Industry Award for her contribution to the development of aviation. In 1931 she and two R.A.F Officers thought of, and carried, the first aeroplane-towed glider airmail.

During the War she was Chief Lady Welfare Officer in Bedfordshire, looking after 20,000 Servicemen and -women. She thought of having a pool of Wedding Dresses at the War Office so a Service Bride could hire a gown for the day.

She bought 1,000 gowns without coupons for the A.T.S., the W.A.A.F.s and the W.R.E.N.S. In 1945 Barbara Cartland received the Certificate of Merit from Eastern Command.

In 1964 Barbara Cartland founded the National Association for Health of which she is the President, as a front for all the Health Stores and for any product made as alternative medicine.

This is now a £65 million turnover a year, with one-third going in export.

In January 1968 she received *La Médaille de Vermeil de la Ville de Paris*. This is the highest award to be given in France by the City of Paris. She has sold 30 million books in France.

In March 1988 Barbara Cartland was asked by the Indian Government to open their Health Resort outside Delhi. This is almost the largest Health Resort in the world.

Barbara Cartland was received with great enthusiasm by her fans, who feted her at a reception in the City, and she received the gift of an embossed plate from the Government.

Barbara Cartland was made a Dame of the Order of the British Empire in the 1991 New Year's Honours List by Her Majesty, The Queen, for her contribution to Literature and also for her years of work for the community.

Dame Barbara has now written 617 books, the greatest number by a British author, passing the 564 books written by John Creasey.

We hope you have enjoyed this Large Print book. Other Chivers Press or G.K. Hall & Co. Large Print books are available at your library or directly from the publishers.

For more information about current and forthcoming titles, please call or write, without obligation, to:

Chivers Press Limited
Windsor Bridge Road
Bath BA2 3AX
England
Tel. (01225) 335336

OR

G.K. Hall & Co.
P.O. Box 159
Thorndike, Maine 04986
USA
Tel. (800) 223–2336

All our Large Print titles are designed for easy reading, and all our books are made to last.